# The Longest Day of the Year

Kim Wright

Balmoral Press
2020

"Dang, but it's hot. Any y'all want a cold drink?"

It's the call of the beach. Four women are sitting on the sand staring out at the ocean, which is coming in faster than expected. Every single one of them knows, girl to woman, that the Carolina tide can be a trickster. You pull your chair down to the edge of the surf, get yourself good and situated and then, just when the shouts of the kids and the cries of the gulls have faded and you're finally starting to relax into your book, here it comes.

All that water, rushing at you out of nowhere. Come to slap you out of the there and then and right back into the here and now. Come to remind you that no matter how many books she crams into a beach bag, no woman can escape the story of her own life. At least not for long.

Not even here on Elliott Point, a sweet little stretch of sand that seems custom-built for escape.

These four women know each other only in that unreal sort of "summer friends" way. They normally wouldn't even take the time to speculate on each other's lives, but heat and boredom tend to make people talk. Throughout the long day, as the sun rises and sinks, casual conversations give way to confessions and, since everyone knows that this whole world officially ends on Labor Day, summer friendships, like summer romances, are the safest kind. You can say whatever you want without that nagging small town fear that your words will someday come boomeranging back to hurt you.

This particular group ranges in age from 22 to 81 and if they didn't happen to be aligned shoulder to shoulder on this little spit of land, a passerby might assume they don't have much in common. The youngest one is just starting to rip open the box of life while the oldest is sealing hers up and the two in between just keep moving stuff around, like you do when you're lost in the middle. But there's one thing they all share and that's how much they love it here. They love the way every day on Elliott Point is just like the one before and how, once you cross the bridge from the mainland and roll down the window to smell the salt water, time ceases to matter. They love how beach life spins itself in circles, so that a woman staring out at the water can lose herself in fantasies of the future and memories of the past and still be exactly here, perfectly here, only and forever here, all in the same breath.

*Anyone could call themselves a goddamn mystic*, Josie thinks, *just as long as they live at the beach.* Using language like that is most emphatically not the way she was raised, but Josie's 59 and peeking over the cliff of sixty is enough to give even a Christian woman a profane turn of mind. Josie doesn't speak this thought out loud because she often cusses without meaning to and who knows, maybe her words would upset the others. Hard to say. Clio claims to be a fully legal 22, old enough to pour drinks in a bar, but if you look her square in the face she could pass for 14 and Amy's 37, which should make her game for anything. But that one's always struck Josie as sort of a priss-pot and a snob, sitting up there in that obscenely big house of hers, literally looking down on the rest of them. Cully must be least a thousand by now, give or take, but she can be a strange one. Sometimes Josie feels like Cully's tough as nails and other times the old woman seems to be unraveling right before her eyes. But either way, Cully's definitely closest to the edge of the cliff and Josie doesn't want the karma of being the one to nudge her the final few inches over. So she figures she needs to keep her goddamns to herself.

"I'm going to die here," Cully murmurs softly, almost as if she's been reading Josie's mind.

"I want to die here," Amy says. "Right here. Sitting this very chair."

"Well then I may as well be a good sport and promise to die here too," Clio says, digging through her beach bag, which is dangling perilously close to the foam. "But first I'm thinking I might want to live here. Anybody know what time it is?"

Cully fishes her iPhone out of her wrinkled cleavage. "3:43."

"Shit. Excuse my French, but shit. I gotta take a shower. I gotta go."

*So the young one can cuss and get away with it,* Josie thinks, which is a relief because ever since the moment of her diagnosis, she hasn't wanted to say anything but "shit" all day long. It's not just that they took her breast and shot her full of chemicals, it's that at the end of six months of pure hell, that child of a doctor had the gall to smile and tell her she'd probably live.

Probably. Now there's a fine word. It's the sort of word that'll shake a woman wide awake at 3 am and it's the one that's sent Josie crawling back to this nowhere little town -seeking healing, seeking forgiveness, seeking a second chance. Salt water cures everything. That's what her grandma used to say. So what's all the water in this ocean good for, after all, if it can't baptize a woman into her own personal second chance?

"Shit," Clio says again, but she still doesn't move. Amy does. She turns in her canvas chair -high quality, expensive, requiring vigilant maintenance, like everything in her life- and looks up toward her house. It's a vaulting sort of thing, with rooms and decks popping off in every direction. The sort of house you'd give a name to if you're the kind of person inclined to give a house a name. Not everybody's that type.

"I need to get moving too," she says. "Time to get the kids some dinner."

Neither Josie nor Cully stir. It's one of the beauties of being old. You might pee when you sneeze and fart when you laugh and you hear 28-year-old doctors use the word "probably" way more than you'd like, but least you don't have to haul yourself out of a perfectly comfortable beach chair and go get anybody their dinner. Well, nobody but yourself and for a woman living alone, dinner's pretty much the easiest thing in the world. Sprinkle a little cereal in a bowl and boom, it's done. It's when you're expected to take care of other people that life starts getting wadded up and sticky.

"I gotta go in, and shower, and get myself all prettied up and get my behind to the Spanish Moss by 4:45," Clio says. "Cut up a thousand oranges and lemons and stick 'em

6

on little skewers with maraschino cherries and scrape the mold out of the ice machine and fold a whole bundle of blue napkins so they stand up all perky like little swans. Ask me if I want to do any of these things. Do I want to? No. But that's what I gotta do."

None of the others bother to answer. They hear some variation of this litany every afternoon. Clio works at one of the most popular seafood shacks on the strand. It's hard work but it's brief work. Four to nine is a typical shift, which means a girl can laze around on the beach all day and party all night and still pull in good tip money from the golfers and fishermen who frequent the place. Aging men and pretty young women. It's the standard recipe for transfers of cash.

And cash is precisely what Clio needs. She needs it more than anything, or at least what she swears, and yet each day at about this time she has a whale of a lot of trouble getting herself moving. Amy is immobilized too, sinking deeper and deeper into the soft sand and wondering if it would be permissible to order in pizza for the second night in a row. Or are they up to the third? The kids would rather have it than anything and she's never claimed to be much of a cook. But there's always the chance Brian would wander in and Brian can be scathing whenever he suspects she's neglecting her motherly duties.

He's a fine one to talk. Summer's supposed to be all about family and yet most nights Brian comes home so late that he winds up sleeping on the couch and that's fine - preferable really- except for the fact that pretty soon the kids are going to start figuring things out. Especially Merry, who's sharp as a knife, and then what's Amy going to say? That Daddy goes off, day after day, night after night, and half the time Mommy doesn't have a country clue as to where he is?

"I hear that boy's truck," Josie says.

"No you don't," says Clio, which makes no sense because nobody can say what another person does or does not hear and besides, there's definitely a truck pulling up from somewhere. The women all stir with a sense of arrival -even Cully, whose command of both sight and sound are becoming sketchier every day.

8

Josie jabs her finger vigorously towards the dunes, in the direction of the row of little cottages that sit in the very shadow of Amy's fine house. "You know darn well that you hear a truck and you know darn well it's your afternoon boy," she says. "That pretty young farmer. What's his name?"

"Dupree," Clio says fretfully. "Now I ask you, what kind of name is Dupree?"

"I've read about this thing called the Hemlock Society," Cully says, "and they know how to mix up something called a poison cocktail. There's stuff in the recipe to help you keep it down long enough to kill you. Because that's the problem with poison, you know. Not getting it in, but keeping it down. The body can't help itself, it automatically fights back."

"It most certainly does," says Josie. "Your body wants to live. So does mine. And what does that tell you?"

Cully breezes on, pretending not hear. "Those Hemlock people won't actually stand there and feed you the cocktail because you know... all the legal stuff. But they'll help you mix it together in the right proportions and they'll film you picking it up and drinking it of your own accord. Then they'll sit there beside you and wait until they're sure you're good and gone. Hold your hand if you ask them. Play you a hymn, or the Beatles. Whatever you want. Seems more than decent of them. Any of ya'll ever heard about that?"

"Hush," Josie says. "Nobody here's fixing to kill themselves. That's crazy talk."

Cully doesn't flinch. "It was on NPR," she says. "NPR isn't crazy talk."

*Sooner or later Merry's going to notice*, Amy thinks. In fact, it's probably already hit her oldest child how little any of them actually see their dad. And then Merry will point this out to the boys and Andrew will start asking questions because that's just what Andrew does. Where the water goes at low tide and if people in China are really going to hell just because they never heard of Jesus and why if Pluto and Goofy are both dogs, Pluto has to live in a dog house while Goofy can stand up and wear clothes and walk around talking just fine. Andrew never lets anything rest and once he gets going Merry'll dig in and argue back and Adam will lurk around like he always does -quiet, tilting his head, looking worried- and Amy has no idea what she's supposed to say about any of it. It's one thing to tell your kids that Mommy doesn't know where Daddy is. It's a whole other thing to tell them Mommy doesn't care.

"You heard that truck as well as I did," Josie says. Clio pushes to her feet.

"Why're you so worried about a truck?" she says. "All I know is that I have to get myself to work."

"He pulls into that driveway the same time every afternoon," Josie says. Her voice has gone down low as a whisper. "A woman could set a clock by him."

"Probably just brought me a cantaloupe," Clio says, at last starting to move toward her cottage and her shower because it truly must be coming up on four by now. "And he doesn't do it every day, just when he's running early on his delivery route. Drops off whatever's not fit to sell. A couple of runty tomatoes or a handful of speckled beans." She leans her head back, squinting up at the cloudless sky. "Now I ask you, what kind of person brings a girl a scratched-up

11

watermelon with a big old white spot on one side?"

"What's on the outside doesn't have anything to do with what's on the inside," Amy says. She's an odd one to make this particular observation, but the others are too sunk in their own thoughts to notice.

"I'll tell you what kind of boy brings a girl those things," Josie finally says to Clio. "A nice one. A good boy who's well on his way to becoming a good man." She poured a beer into a water bottle before she came out, even though such subterfuge is pointless. Sure, the open carry of alcohol is forbidden- this is the South and a family beach, after all, and don't even get her going on all the silly rules about liquor sales on Sunday- but only one lone lifeguard is visible and he's stationed halfway to the pier. With so much shoreline to cover, if a swimmer did go under all he'd be able to do is wave goodbye. Josie looks up at Clio, who's still staring out over the water, not even making a move to gather up her stuff. "And when you get a little older you'll see that a good man is a rare thing. A woman can go her whole long lifetime and only find two or three."

"The trouble with this country," Cully rasps, her voice gone thick from the spray, "is that it's too expensive to live and they won't let you die. I already told my children I won't go into one of those homes. Once the Medicare doctors get ahold of you..."

"Oh, come on, Cully, Josie's right," says Amy. "You just need to hush. I've seen you coming over those dunes in the morning, carrying your easels and your canvas and that big old fishing box full of paints. Hell, woman, you've got twenty good years left in you. You're tougher than the rest of us combined."

"Every single one of you is managing to miss the point," Clio says. "The point is that Dupree only brings me whatever the restaurants won't take, and then he expects me to give him a curtsy and a 'much obliged, kind sir.' Damn, Josie. You know all that as good as I do. And yet you think it's my job to stand there day after day, batting my eyes and thanking him for bringing me a squashed tomato or a squashed squash or whatever it is that somebody stepped on while they were loading the truck?"

"Money isn't everything," Amy says. Which is another fine observation coming from her, but it seems like people most often preach the sermon they need to hear.

"Oh yeah," Clio says slowly, and then she shakes the last drops of a warm beer into the foam. "Money ain't everything. That's what people with money always say."

Josie turns to study Amy's house with all its domes and decks and cupolas, which she's always thought looks like a wedding cake left to melt in the sun. On some level she can see why Clio would be exasperated. Amy's the only one of them who can claim any real security, who has any real roots, and yet she's always yammering on about the limitations of the material world. The unhappiness of a middle-aged trophy wife - while undoubtedly real enough- is nothing but annoying to the young and broke or the old and scared. Sometimes Josie wonders why Amy even bothers sitting out here every day with the rest of them. Surely she's busy, with three growing kids in her house. Surely she has a whole pile of rich, well-manicured friends closer to her own age.

"I heard of a woman who moved into one of those assisted living places and they kept the rest of her alive after her heart stopped," Cully mumbles. "Just so the home could keep drawing her social security check, month after month. Can you imagine what that feels like? To have your heart stop and your brain just go on and on and on, not even knowing that you're dead?"

"You must have heard that part wrong," snaps Clio, using both hands to pull her beach chair out of the sand. It takes a good effort to dislodge it, the jerk of the thing nearly pulling her off her feet. "Or else you dreamed it. Nobody can live without a heart."

*Of course they can,* thinks Josie. *A woman can live without a heart for years. Decades. For a lifetime, if she has to. God, but these girls are young.*

Amy looks around blinking, as if surprised at the sudden discord that's sprung up among the group. Some days it seems like they get along better when they don't talk out loud. "Cully, honey, please stop with all this nonsense about nursing homes and cocktails made out of hemlock," she says.

15

"You're going to outlive us all. You'll dance on our graves. Won't she, Josie?"

But Josie is watching Clio, who has a pack of cigarettes stuck down the front of her bathing suit top and the empty beer can crammed under one armpit and no suntan lotion anywhere in sight. Still living like a kid, thinking tomorrow's never going to come, and she starts to reach out, to touch Clio's leg and tell her to be careful with it all. To be careful with her strong young body that she leaves lying around like a doll, flopping it down first one place and then the other, and to be careful with the chances life is giving her. There's a sort of holy grace that only comes to a girl early in life, way before she even knows what it means, and then, when she's old and would welcome even one of those chances, the bitter joke is that they're gone for good.

Chances like that sweet farmer boy waiting patiently by Clio's front door with the best watermelon of the whole crop in his hands.

Because Josie can see it all, she can see Clio's whole story. See it as clearly as she's watching a movie on a screen. She lifts a palm to stop the girl from the foolishness she's about to rush into- or at least slow her down. But Clio brushes by Josie as if she's not even there.

\*\*\*\*

The cottage is a dump.

You don't believe me? Perhaps you've been charmed by the descriptions of the previous scene or maybe your own memories of long ago summers at the beach? Well, let me tell you precisely how bad this place is.

You can't even open the screen door. The hinges rusted off three storms ago, so what you have to do is pick it up and move it away from the house. Clio grabs the wooden frame in both hands, sets it aside with a gentle grunt and steps through the opening. Then she turns and wrestles the door back, aligning it as best she can, hoping to keep at least some of the skeeters and horseflies out.

Dupree's precisely where she expected him to be, sitting at her kitchen table, waiting. Everybody calls him by his last name. Most of the restaurants on the strand just view him as whatever son or nephew or cousin happens to be driving the truck this summer and making the deliveries from Dupree Farms. Half a dozen tall sun-bleached farmboys have come and gone through the years, all of them answering to nothing more specific than "Dupree." Clio supposes the particular Dupree parked at her kitchen table must have a first name of some kind but the only time she asked he seemed funny about saying it out loud so she never pushed the point.

"Maybe I'll just call you Rumpelstiltskin," she'd said, but he'd only frowned.

Not much of a surprise there. Clio's used to people not having the slightest idea what she's talking about, probably because she's one of those girls who grew up eating books like candy, waiting all month for the last Saturday, because that was when the Bookmobile parked in the Piggly Wiggly lot from ten to three. There were rules back in those days. You could only get four books at a time and you had to check them out by writing their Dewey decimal numbers on a slip of paper, using one of those squat little pencils like they give you at the putt-putt places. Clio used to take four easy ones the first time through, books way below her grade level, then she'd sit and read them fast on the curb in the shade of the shopping carts, so that she could go back and get four harder ones to see her through the long weeks ahead. Hell, one time when she wasn't much more than ten she'd even taken it upon her skinny gap--toothed self to check out The Iliad. When the bookmobile librarian had tried to talk her out of such a mad plan, Clio had just jerked her chin and taken The Odyssey as well. Coming from a trailer park didn't mean she was stupid.

So Clio can understand a boy like Dupree wanting to reinvent himself. She knows why he hides behind the anonymity of that family name, keeping his head ducked low and his voice pitched even lower, why he plays so fast and loose with the particulars of his personal past. She understands better than anybody how it feels to be one person on the mainland and to become somebody completely different the minute you drive across the bridge to the beach.

Dupree pushes the pack of Salems across the table, but Clio shakes her head.

"I've got to take a shower," she says. "There's beer in the fridge if you want one." Which is kind of a bitchy thing to say because he's already gotten himself a Miller and it's sitting there on the table plain as day beside his cigarettes.

Dupree just grins at her and says "Darling, I thought you'd never ask." He's like Cully in that way. It's damn near impossible to piss him off.

But dear God is he pretty. Josie got that much right. When he squints those steel blue eyes, with the smoke curling up from his narrow lips he looks like James Dean, courtesy of Giant, sitting in that old Cadillac roadster with the brim of a straw hat pulled over his brow. And while Clio knows that Elliott Point's answer to James Dean is approximately the last thing in the world a girl like her needs to be wasting her time on, somehow this country boy ends up sitting, day after day, at her kitchen table. Drinking her beer and smoking her cigarettes and there's not really a word in the English language fully suitable for what the two of them are to each other.

Nobody at the Spanish Moss can know they're messing around like this. It would ruin everything. Knock her right back down that ladder she's spent a lifetime trying to climb and Clio's not about to let that happen. This little rented cottage might be falling down around her ears. It might have a rain tank porch shower and three of the five front steps rotted clean through and a screen door that won't properly shut, much less lock, but she's gotten herself down here on her own, dammit, three seasons in a row, and she's taken as much root as a girl can in this sandy soil. Clio calls it her secret, which is funny because pretty much anybody who's ever talked to her for five minutes knows it, but all she's ever wanted to do is live right here, at this very beach. To have a big old fuck-you kinda house with a view that stretches all the way to the point. She can almost picture it in her mind and she's may not be particularly close to getting this dream but she's closer than she's ever been before and she's not going to let anybody snatch it away from her. Not Dupree with his James Dean sneer -hell, not James Dean

21

himself, even if he found a way to dig out of his grave and growl "Hey girl, how 'bout it?"

"Built you a sandcastle while I was waiting," he says. "Out there beside the steps. Did you see it?"

She shakes her head.

"Bet you stepped right over it." He takes a sip of his beer. "Hell, you probably stepped on it."

Clio reaches for her terrycloth robe, the one she keeps hanging on a peg in the kitchen.

"You're going to have to 'cuse me for my umpteen sins, kind sir," she says. "But right now I gotta shower."

Dupree cuts his eyes. "Want some company?"

"Not particularly." A breeze blows through the open kitchen window. One of those sharp clear blasts of ocean air that can make a girl shudder even on the hottest day of the year. "I wouldn't describe myself as particularly seeking company, but you know...I mean, it ain't like the lock works."

And then they both laugh, because they know damn well he'll follow her out there on the porch within five minutes. Naked as a pair of jaybirds, the sun beating down from above and the pulses of tank water raining down cold as midnight and that contrast, jumping from hot to cold and then back again, is as close to ecstasy as a pair of dirt road kids like them have any right to expect.

And here's another thing they know damn well. That there's a perfectly good word for what they're doing together, even if it's the sort of word that both of their Grandmas, being good Baptists, taught them never to say out loud.

****

When you've got kids, every single minute can cost you. Amy starts in about ten minutes after Clio, bracing herself for reentry as she weaves her way among the dunes.

The girl's the problem. She's fourteen and a fourteen-year-old girl is always mad about something. God knows what it'll be on this

23

particular day, but it'll be something. It's a bitter sort of joke that the girl's name is Merry, a trait she hasn't exhibited for at least two years, not since adolescence blew in like one of those late summer hurricanes. Now every afternoon is punctuated with sighs and sulks and slamming doors.

The twins are easier. They're barely nine, and standing mother to boys is mostly a matter of driving in a big loop between schools and soccer fields and swimming pools and throwing food at them every hour on the hour. There's a sweetness to Amy's boys too -the way they turn into toddlers again whenever they're sleepy, curling up beside her on the couch as they watch ball games or Nickelodeon, their bodies warm and smooth. Adam and Andrew still let her touch them. Merry hasn't submitted to a cuddle in years.

Amy rises through her house and the elevator doors open to the smell of bacon. That's no surprise since BLTs are one of the few foods Andrew can manage and she's left them alone for almost three hours, which in boy-time is a span of two meals. Amy walks through the kitchen, grabbing a rogue napkin and wiping the counter as she goes, moving the cast iron frying pan to the sink, her beach bag still slung over one shoulder. A brand new jar of mayonnaise is sitting on the counter.

Apparently the boys tried to get into it and couldn't. Amy gives it a twist and when that doesn't work she raps the lid against the countertop a few times. Not the slightest budge. She goes to the stairs and calls up to the third floor. The playroom floating two levels above her is a young boy's dream - table tennis, billiards, darts and a few nights ago their dad brought home an old Pong machine from God-knows-where and showed them how to play. Adam and Andrew are obsessed with it, up there whacking that little blip of a ball back and forth at all hours of the day and night.

It bugs Amy when she stops to think about it. Here they've moved heaven and earth to build the finest house on three consecutive beaches, and her kids hardly ever put a foot on the sand. A collection of outside toys is crammed in a laundry basket in the corner of the kitchen, just under a lone chalkboard, evidently intended by some long-gone decorator to keep grocery lists or gay welcoming messages for visitors coming in for the weekend. The basket holds frisbees, bak-a-ball, croquet mallets. castle molds, dive masks, the bent frame of a kite. Amy picks up a piece of chalk and writes GO OUTSIDE! PLAY! and draws an arrow toward the toys. She stands back, adds the word NOW! then walks over to push open the double French doors that lead to the main deck.

It's not the best view the house offers. Not even close. Amy and Brian have built themselves four stories, start to finish, not including the observation deck on the absolute top, complete with a telescope for stargazing, even though Amy has only climbed there once, on the day they moved in. She has a type of vertigo. It comes and goes, depending on her mood. The staircase leading to upper levels shoots through the open vaulting space of the great room and considering that even the first floor of the house hovers twenty feet in the air, Amy had spent her first and only trip to the observation deck clutching the rail and trying not to think about exactly how high off the ground she was.

Of course the kids had loved it on sight. Merry had started spinning the telescope round and round, and Adam was daring Andrew to cannonball off the railing into the small turquoise square of pool below.

"You could make it," he said. "If you had the guts to jump."

"You first, then I will," Andrew had said.

"Sure," said Adam. "Because I have to do everything first. Even be born." He had looked down then, squinted at the perfect pool waiting below and laughed. "I could do it," he said. "Anybody could."

"Don't be silly," Amy had said, holding onto their thin little shoulders. Supposedly to steady them, but mostly to steady herself. She may have stood right there smiling and nodding while the architect had drawn it up but the bottom line was she hated this much altitude. It made the whole world spin. "Neither one of you is jumping off of any kind of deck. Nobody is. So hush."

And then Andrew -he's the sweet one- had said "But you and Daddy can get me life insurance." He'd asked for it more than once before, whenever those stupid Gerber baby commercials came on TV, which Amy had always thought was weird. The day they'd moved into the beach house had been the first time she understood that he thought if you had life insurance it meant you couldn't die.

"Baby," she'd said. "Oh, my sweet boy, there's no piece of paper on earth that'll make a person live forever." But then Adam had tried to pull the telescope away from Merry, either to look at some sailboat in the distance or, who knows, maybe a girl in a bikini because Andrew got all the innocence for both of them. Andrew got all the innocence the world is prepared to give and Adam's the one who's solid, the one who likes sports and math and girls in bikinis and Amy knows by instinct he won't ever give her any real trouble. He's the one who she'll probably never have a real conversation with but who will take her in forty years from now when she breaks a hip or forgets her name.

"Then why do people get life insurance?" Andrew had asked her. He was frowning that frown he often gets. The one that indicates he thinks this grownup world he's being slowly and steadily nudged toward makes zero sense. And he's right about that part, but there's no point in telling him that just yet.

"You buy life insurance so that somebody else will get money when you die," she'd said. "Somebody you love more than yourself. Somebody you want to make sure will be fine even after you're dead." Then she'd turned away from his bewildered, freckled face to wrest the telescope from the other two kids. Why had she and Brian insisted on four stories in the first place? Why had they built a house that took them all higher than any happy family had the need to be?

Amy sighs now and pulls herself back from the railing. It looks like Josie and Cully are still on the beach. They just nudged their chairs closer together when the younger women left and they seem to be talking hard about something, leaning in so close their foreheads are nearly touching. Lucky them, not to have a responsibility in the world and lucky Clio too, because judging by the sound of running water coming from the small grey cottage below, she seems to be taking a shower.

Clio's rental may a tumbledown affair, but it does have one absolute pleasure -an outdoor shower, perched right on the edge of the porch. The collected rainwater comes out as cold as sweet tea in April and warm as coffee by August but either way, nothing feels better than to walk up from the beach sticky and hot and find your towel and shampoo and bathrobe waiting so that you can get yourself clean before you come into the house. Amy leans over the deck, the railing cutting into her side, but she can't see into the shower, not from this angle, and she's not sure what particular perversity is even causing her to try. God knows, they all heard Dupree's truck rattling up. No point in pretending like they didn't. He was probably waiting on those rotted steps for Clio to come off the beach like she does the same time every day and he probably snuck into the shower with her. They're most likely having sex standing up under the water. What do you call that? A knee trembler? Clio acts like she doesn't care a fig about him but everybody knows she does. Probably even loves him, although "love" can be a skittish word. Runs sideways like a crab and sometimes gets away from you just when you think you're close enough to grab it, pinchers and all.

Amy closes her eyes and tries to recapture the memory. What raw hot afternoon sex smells and sounds like, what it feels like to be in a shower with a man. Or out in the dunes at midnight. Heck, the back of a flatbed truck will work in a pinch, but everybody knows that kind of passion fades once you're married. A bit of settling down is to be expected. It's actually a good sign, proof of your commitment, and besides, it's not like either she or Brian makes that much effort anymore. Half the time she really is asleep before he gets home and the other half she lunges for the light the minute she hears the sharp roar of his engines turning down the driveway. She doesn't like it when he comes in smelling like scotch and cigars. It's the sort of stench that cologne only makes worse.

What's happening between them, this slow drifting apart. The giving in and giving up. Amy knows it's partly her fault. And partly isn't.

"What're you looking at?"

Merry has come through the doors and is standing right behind her, looking down at the cottage. Amy jerks back from the railing.

*I'm spying at a young couple in an outdoor shower,* she thinks. *And I'm trying to remember what sex feels like, especially with a man you think you love.*

But of course she doesn't say that. Merry's evidently just come from a bath of her own. Her long brown hair is wet and tangled and a towel is draped around her shoulders. She's frowning.

"And why do you have a jar of mayonnaise in your hand?"

"I think the boys tried to open it for BLTs but they couldn't. And I can't either."

"Jesus." Merry takes the little glass jar and pops the lid with one decisive twist. "Why do you even buy this kind when you know half the time you can't get it open?"

"Because any southerner worth her salt keeps a jar of Duke's in kitchen. Back in the day, my grandmother even put it cakes."

"She did not."

"I assure you that she did. It's a country trick. A big old dollop of Duke's mayonnaise, right in the batter. Keeps your cake moist."

Merry pauses to consider this. "Miracle Whip's better."

"Go wash your mouth out, young lady."

Merry shrugs. For some reason she's gazing toward the porch of the little cottage too, although she can't have a clue there's a shower there, much less what's going on underneath the water. "Daddy likes Miracle Whip too. I guess I get it from him."

Amy strains to listen above the wind. Has the sound of running water stopped? Or was anyone ever in the shower in the first place? *I'm jealous of Clio,* she thinks, *which is completely ridiculous since the only thing in the world Clio wants is my life. All of it, right here. This deck, these kids, the status she imagines comes with a certain kind of husband, the right last name. She thinks I'm the lucky one, and maybe I am. I can't let myself get too sentimental about what goes on in a porch shower on a hot summer afternoon. Youth is never as much fun as you remember. Neither is poverty.*

"Did you hear me?" says Merry. "I'm saying that maybe I'm more like my daddy."

"No," says Amy. "Not really."

"Well, I think so."

Amy's so preoccupied that for a moment she forgets she's afraid of her own daughter. "Then I guess you're going to have to go ahead and think so."

A bit of a pause then. Her mother ordinarily rushes to comfort and console, so the girl isn't sure how to take even the slightest degree of push back. Finally Merry gives another shrug, more elaborate than the first. "Now that the jar's open you better put it in the refrigerator. Salmonella and stuff."

"Good God," says Amy. "Salmonella? What business do you have using a word like that? When I wasn't much more than your age I used to keep an open jar of Duke's and one of those little sharp church lady knives in the glove compartment of my Mustang all summer and I never started out anywhere without a loaf of white bread on the back

34

seat. That way when I got hungry I could pull off whatever road I was driving and pick a tomato from the garden of an obliging farmer and make myself a little lunch."

"You did not. That's worse than icing a cake with mayonnaise."

"You didn't put the Duke's on the cake like icing, silly. You put it in the batter before you cooked it. And keeping the fixings for sandwiches in their cars was how broke people used to travel. You want to know something else? It wasn't so bad."

Merry is thinking. "What's a church lady knife?"

"Oh, you know. Those little silver ones with a fine blade. A paring knife, they call them, and church ladies used to sell them to raise money for their projects. Orphans in Kenya and seat cushions for the sanctuary, that kind of thing."

"I thought church ladies sold cookbooks with casserole recipes."

"Those too." Amy stretches and looks back toward the older two women sitting on the beach. "I used to drive that car bare-footed and back then if a girl had herself a little church lady knife and a jar of Duke's and a loaf of Wonder Bread and two dollars worth of gas, the world was hers. I could've gone all the way across the country like that, if I'd ever needed to."

"You're lying. You didn't live off hot mayonnaise and stolen tomatoes for a whole summer. You'd be dead."

"That's the summer I met your Daddy."

"God, Mom. Why are you always so determined to act like a redneck?"

Amy pauses. Tries to choose her next words carefully. "Baby, all I'm trying to tell you is that it doesn't take nearly as much to make a girl happy as you seem to think it does."

But Merry still isn't convinced. "Daddy says building this house was your idea."

****

The coconut aroma of someone's sunscreen, another person's stale beer. That ugly-sweet stench of a headless fish tossed to the shore and the salty air ruffling her hair. Josie sits back and breathes it all in, then turns to Cully.

"Do you know what day this is?"

Cully hesitates. "Friday?"

"Well, yeah, of course, but my point is that it's June 21. The longest day of the year."

"That too."

"I thought maybe you'd forgotten the date."

"Not much chance of that."

Josie stretches. "How many summers would you figure the two of us have sat here on this same beach talking?"

Cully seems preoccupied and doesn't give the question much consideration. "I don't know. Plenty. You've always been my favorite."

"Now that surprises me."

"But I don't remember you being such a whiner."

*You've never known me sick,* Josie thinks. *You've never known me scared.* She can't sit still today. She's twitching and squirming and finally she turns again and looks back at the two houses behind her. The unhappy mansion perched over the dunes, the little broken down love nest burrowed among them. One of them dominates the skyline while the roof of the other one is barely visible over the mounds of sand.

"What do you think our girl's up there doing?" Josie asks Cully, twisting back into her seat just in time to catch a wave, straight to the chest. The water's colder than it has any right to be on the official start of summer.

Cully chuckles. "What are young girls always doing? The wrong thing. But you're not going to save her from any of it, so get that thought right out of your head."

"I'll tell you what I'm afraid of. I'm afraid she's so impressed by that rich boy who's chasing her that she'll wind up letting him make her ashamed of where she came from. I used to be the same way, you know. Too eager to please. Willing to flat-out lie, if it came to that. My Grandma had this term.

'Getting above your raising,' she called it. 'Doesn't do a girl any good to get above her raising.' But I tried. I tried for years to be something that I wasn't, and I'm ashamed of that now." Josie blinks back the sudden tears." Have I ever told you about my Grandma? She was a good solid woman. Could wring a chicken's neck with one hand and with the other one turn out needlework so fine it'd make an angel weep. Have I ever told you I was named after her? Only I let some trifling man make me forget that. For a while."

Cully sighs. Favorite or not, sometimes Josie wears her out. "Seems to me every woman in the world has let some trifling man or another pull her down in the ditch and thanked him for the fall. You've just had one? Count yourself lucky. Now, what on God's green earth is your point?"

"Only that it's hard to...it's hard to watch her walk straight into a trap and not at least try and stop her."

"You've got kids. And they're grown, right?"

"Well sure. At least in the numerical sense of the word."

Cully's gaze remains fixed on the sea. "Then you know damn well that the main lesson we've come to learn in this lifetime is how to let go. Figure out when to stand back, shut up, and let fate take its course. Our girl up there has gotta make her own mistakes. Gotta fall into her own messes and spend as many years as it takes rolling around in them. And then, in her own sweet time, she'll figure out how to pull herself up and move on."

Josie sighs and settles back in her chair. "Which one of them are we talking about, anyway? Clio or Amy?"

Cully chuckles again. "Doesn't matter. Both of them have plenty of time."

\*\*\*

Clio can remember when she thought that shrimp were something exotic. A resort food. The kind of thing tourists and rich girls ate.

But now she's sick of the very sight of them. If you get in thirty minutes early for your shift at the Spanish Moss, you can pick out anything you want from the kitchen and have yourself a feast. Her first summer down, when she walked around half-starved all the time, Clio had taken them up on the offer every single day she was scheduled to work and by the end of June she'd eaten her way through the whole menu -not just shrimp but crabcakes and clam strips and scallops and of course flounder, which was the catch of the day every day. But if a girl waits tables in a fry shack, it doesn't take long for the romance to seafood to die.

Prepping the morning haul is brutal, stinky work. The kitchen floor is concrete and slopes toward a drain in the corner so they can hose the whole thing down at the start of the shift. Fish scales and shrimp tails and flat glassy eyes clump together and clog the metal grate, collectively looking like some sort of monster from a children's picture book. Clio picks her way across the sticky floor to the heating bin, where she grabs a foil-wrapped baked potato from the pile and, bouncing it back and forth between her palms, she moves to the row of cabinets. Digs out a scarred plastic plate, splits open the steaming pouch and drenches the whole thing in cocktail sauce.

Then, with a quick glance at the clock, she carries it out to the bar where Jeannie is already halfway through her prep. Wiping down the beer glasses one at a time with a soft cloth, and while the girl talks too much, Clio considers Jeannie an okay person. I mean, Jeanne calls Clio "Cli-baby" for some weird reason, giving her a nickname on top of a nickname, and she calls the owner's son "Jack" based on his alleged resemblance to President Kennedy. It's all silly, but Clio knows Jeannie's just looking for a way to fit in and she was like that herself the first summer. New girls always try too hard. Besides, Jeannie's not completely off on the Jack thing. The owner's son doesn't look particularly like a Kennedy in the face but he does have the same reckless air of the young president. That same sense of roadster convertibles and tennis rackets and white cable knit summer sweaters slung over one shoulder.

Clio had never heard of such a thing as a summer sweater until she started working at the Spanish Moss. You sure as hell don't need a summer sweater in South Carolina, but this so-called Jack said he'd bought his in Massachusetts, a place where evidently it's cold even when it's hot. Her first season at the Spanish Moss, when she was shy and the two of them barely spoke, Clio had heard Jack make noises to the other serving girls about getting a whole new wardrobe when he was at Harvard. But by the second summer, when she knew her business better, she'd flat out confronted him about it, and he'd backed right down.

No, he hadn't exactly gone to school at Harvard he'd told her, ducking his head so that a lock of light brown hair fell across his high, elegant forehead. But he'd applied there. Got as far as taking the campus tour. Bought the sweater from some gift shop in Cambridge and then came home and enrolled in the University of South Carolina, just like his daddy and granddaddy and two uncles before him. That whole Ivy League college tour had proven to be nothing more than one of those pipe dreams, a foolish idea he'd gotten as a kid or maybe from watching a movie. Something his mama had encouraged and his daddy had scoffed at and the end -well in the end, Daddy was the one who wrote the checks.

Jack had confessed all this sort of sheepishly, his eyes down and his face flushed as he talked, but the truth is that she'd liked him all the better for pretending to be a Harvard man.

Telling a lie like that showed ambition. She had ambition too. In this sense, Clio had wanted Jack from the very first moment she saw him. But no...that may be the most dramatic way to say it, but it's not quite right. It would be truer to say that Clio had wanted Jack even before she saw him. Wanted him from the first moment she'd known he existed, that the owner of the Spanish Moss had such a son. He'd still been at the state university when she'd first driven down over her spring break of her senior year of high school, determined to get herself some sort of job at the beach. Then Memorial Day had come, the start of the season, but he still wasn't there.

Word was he'd gone somewhere to "crew." Clio hadn't been entirely sure what crewing meant but it sounded rich, and her ears had perked up that first summer. She'd taken a working girl's pleasure in just hearing the stories, seeing his blurry, indistinct face in the family pictures hanging on the wood-paneled wall behind the cash register. She would stand sometimes when they weren't busy, scanning the sequence of photos and watching him growing up like all of us do, a year at a time. Crawling, toddling, running, throwing a softball in one picture, catching a fish in another. Wearing a red and white checked shirt while leaning over a set of oars, squinting into the morning sun. Standing in a suit, looking solemn. Maybe he was at somebody's funeral, or a wedding. But the point was he'd stepped out of the receiving line just a bit and was standing apart from his two brothers. Distinguishing himself as the special one, even then.

It's easy for a girl to spin a fantasy about a boy when she has just that much to go on - nothing but a verb like "crewing" and a toothy smile, not to mention the promise of relatives considerate enough to die and leave you piles of money. It wasn't just that Jack's daddy owned the Spanish Moss, which may not be much to look at, but which is surely what Clio's own daddy would call a cash cow. Maybe it was the fact that Valerie the bartender kept saying that the boss was buying up land left and right, all over the beach. She told Clio that Jack's family were people on the move and who was Clio to argue? Valerie was one of the very few locals at the Spanish Moss, born at the hospital two miles inland and Valerie knew everything. She'd stuck her head out from behind the wall of beer spigots and mouthed "developments," and even gullible first-summer-at-the-beach Clio, sitting there with her country ways and a platterful of free shrimp, could figure out what that meant. Shopping centers and fancy restaurants with wine lists in a book separate from the menu and ceiling to floor windows with high silent views of the water. Zoning hearings and seats on the town council and newspaper clippings of people cutting ribbons stretched across freshly-painted parking lots.

Only a fool of a girl wouldn't want herself a piece of that.

And people have called Clio many things in her life, but nobody's ever called her a fool.

That had been her first summer down, the rough year. The one Clio had spent ironing one-dollar bills and washing out her white denim shorts every night because she only owned that one cute pair. She'd had two roommates and one of them was fat and snored and the other one was a diabetic who'd used her hypodermic needles to shoot vodka into oranges. That girl walked around drunk all the livelong time, even on Wednesday mornings, but by the second summer Clio had arrived back at the restaurant to the immediate and most welcome news that this time Jack would be down at the coast the whole season. His daddy had cracked the whip, Valerie whispered. He only had two more years of college, after all, and it was high time for him to learn the family business. Even if at this point the family business was mostly just concrete pilings and fish heads and empty lots with billboards promising Yankees a piece of the good life.

Clio had stood there, now all of twenty years old but in possession of three cute pairs of shorts and a fully hatched plan. It had felt like the universe was splitting open. For the first time, life was offering her a small sliver of a chance.

She worked on Jack all that summer and the one that followed. Figuring out when to lean toward him. Figuring out when to pull back. And then finally, the year he was a senior, they courted through the fall and winter too -him from his frat house in Columbia and her writing letters from her mama's trailer, making up stories about a life that didn't exist. Classes of her own and dances she never went to. A whiff of romance with a boy she based off some actor in a movie. Just enough detail to make him jealous, to keep him interested, but never enough to make him think she was anything but available for that golden day when he'd come back to the beach, ascend the throne, and take claim to the kingdom his daddy had built for him.

Because when he did, Clio planned to be by his side.

\*\*\*\*

This glorious, magazine-shoot life that they're building depends on one thing: the condo development going up on the point. Everything they own is tied up in it and the investors, Amy's husband among them, swear that when it's approved -and it will be approved, it must be approved- the return will be tremendous. Staggering. It'll jack up real estate prices all up and down the beach, even the little shacks. A high-rise built around a multiuse community will finally put Elliott Point on the map.

But the problem is, the problem is...

The problem is that not everybody wants to put Elliott Point on the map. A development perched right at the end of the peninsula will block the view of every house behind it, including Amy's own. What is it Cully always says?

When you change the view, you change the beach.

Amy's gaze drifts out to the spot where the older women are perched on a diminishing strip of sand. Josie has stood up and is trying to pull her chair out of the tide suck but Cully seems determined to stay right where she is until the end of time. Based on the way they live, Amy suspects that neither of them has a lot of money. They have more than Clio but less than her and a burst of growth all along the beach, an acceleration in land prices...A boom like that could change their lives almost as much as it'll change hers.

Which means, when you stand back and stop and think about it, Josie and Cully and maybe even Clio should be grateful for what Amy's husband is doing. She's the one who has the power to lift their lives to a higher plane. A beach can't all be about sea turtles nesting and gritty roads so rarely traveled that children can scamper back and forth without looking for cars and property values so low any trifling lowlife can afford a cottage. Right now, Elliott Point is a little hidden jewel. The proverbial diamond in the rough. But at some point somebody has to dig down and pull that jewel into the light.

Brian tells her she's crazy for worrying so much about what other people think. He explains -very slowly, as if talking to a small and not particularly bright child- that a certain sort of person will always fight progress. Change scares most people, he says. Scares them so bad they don't even stop to consider if the change in question is for the worst or for the better. Right now their house is the only big one among the cottages but once the condos go in down at the point, who knows? It's a given that more developments will follow. Maybe even hotels. And then all the people who are now snubbing them in the grocery store? The ones who showed up at the town council meeting last week yelling about tradition and sewage? They'll be dancing in the newly-paved street when they see how much money their houses are worth. In the meantime Amy just has to ignore the side eye and the snide little comments, even if they're coming from people she's known for years.

All of which is easy for him to say. Every friend he has is on the development board. Hell, those guys probably go rock hard at the very sound of a word like "progress." Brian's not the one who has to sit on the beach with a clump of women who have loved this place since they were girls.

The kitchen phone rings. Amy pulls herself away from the deck and goes in, leaving the doors agape even though Brian is always telling the kids he isn't working this hard just to air-condition the whole beach. She puts the now-open jar of Duke's on the counter and picks up the phone, her eyes on the take-out menus stuck to the fridge with magnets. Maybe there's another council meeting tonight, or something like that. Something that means Brian won't be home, so pizza would be okay. The boys like it and Merry doesn't count, because Merry doesn't like anything.

"Hello?"

Dead silence.

"Hello?" she repeats. "Who's there?"

Phone service on the point is spotty. A fair number of calls get dropped so Amy waits, expecting a dial tone. But after a second or two of continued silence she realizes there's nothing wrong with the connection. Someone is definitely on the other end. They just aren't speaking.

"Hello," she says again, this time more sharply. "Who is this?"

A voice. Breathy and muffled but definitely female. "Your husband-"

Amy waits. Her heart is beginning to pound. Sure, she's gotten looks in the supermarket, painful pauses in the middle of a conversation, and then there was that sign saying KEEP ELLIOTT PURE very pointedly stuck in the dunes at the exact place where she has to walk right past it with her beach chair every morning. But so far no one has been bold enough to call her house. The place where she lives with her kids. Her eyes blur a little. They're moving into a new era. One where she can be accosted even within her carefully built kingdom. The air around her feels very still. The only thing she can hear is the muted beeping of the game the boys are playing upstairs.

"My husband what?"

It's most likely an environmentalist. Brian says they're the worse. Some nut from somewhere up north, calling to explain how the local ecosystem can't handle a thousand new residents or that driving pilings for a high rise will make the marsh beds unstable. Both of which are probably true, but what the hell is Amy supposed to do about any of it?

She should hang up. She will hang up. But just before she does, the breathy little voice speaks again.

"Your husband is having an affair."

\*\*\*\*

*This water,* Cully thinks. *It never changes, even if everything else does.*

\*\*\*\*

Josie can feel the grit of the sand on the floor as she walks into the kitchen of her cottage. She needs to go into town later and buy a broom, along with ketchup and Tilex and toilet paper and butter and light bulbs and the 112 things you have to get when you're setting up a new place.

But for now she may as well finish unpacking the boxes she's brought from Charlotte and make a grocery list, even knowing that with a pantry this empty she's bound to forget something and have to go back tomorrow and maybe even the day after that. She flips on the TV to keep her company as she starts in on the first box and it goes right to the channel where she left it. One of those DIY shows she kept on in the background as she tried to drift off last night. Yesterday had been rough, serving up one shock after another, and her sleep hasn't been worth a shit lately.

The painting teacher's voice is soft and droning, almost a lullaby. Where does public TV find these guys? They all seem stoned. This one is helping a student with a landscape. Josie looks at the screen just long enough to see that the woman being featured on this episode isn't much of an artist, bless her heart. Bless her heart. That ultimate southern put down, and Josie knows that despite everything she's been through in the last year -despite the diagnosis and the chemo and the fact her hair fell out, stayed out, and finally came back grey- that the pettiness hasn't been completely blasted out of her soul. She can take maybe a two-second look at this woman -who has way more heart than Josie'll ever have because at least she's trying, not just walking around a rented cottage saying that someday she'll pull her shit together and really do something...Josie can look right at this woman and make fun of her for having a late-in-life dream, even though she of all people should know better.

Cancer should make you kinder. Otherwise it's got no purpose at all, if the pain can't teach you something, and it hasn't even been six months since Josie was lying on a gurney in the hall outside of Imaging, parked under an AC vent and trembling from the Freon. Okay, trembling with fear- that's more like it. Fear of a tiny little lump that was apparently enough to stop a whole big body, and the only real surprise was how much, when push came to shove, Josie found she still cared about her own existence. Against all odds she found herself ready to fight to keep this particular soul tucked inside of this particular body, so she'd pulled the thin sheet tighter around her, squeezed her eyes shut and started negotiating with every spirit she could summon. Christian, Hindu, Rastafarian or Navaho- if you have cancer, trust me, you don't give a shit, you start calling on them all.

*Let me live,* she had begged. *Just give me one single perfect year and I swear I'll never be petty again.*

So much for that lie. She'd lived, but she still has moments of pointless cruelty -her reaction to this painting show stands proof of that. She'd come out of that hospital with a scar shaped like a question mark and at first the questions that haunted her were only the most obvious ones: *Did they get it all? Will I live?* But over the last few months her doubts have gradually expanded. *Forget one perfect year. How many imperfect years do I really have left? And what in the name of sweet Jesus am I supposed to do with them?*

So now, even when Josie tries to forget, she can't. The universal symbol of doubt has been carved into her body. She's always hated the word "survivor" and she gets annoyed by the support groups. Her doctors had pretty much insisted she try and she did go once, but the leader had told the circle of women that their wounds were blessings, the broken places where the light comes in. Everybody else had oohed and aahed and clapped but Josie's not capable of that kind of pretending. She'll never be grateful for the loss. She's not interested in breaking open and welcoming holy light, at least not this much, and she's begun to suspect that the wisdom of living in the present moment has been greatly exaggerated. No matter how hard she tries, she can't bring herself to see the blessing in any of this, even though she does recognize that she wouldn't have ever come back to this little beach, unless that young doctor hadn't sat down and shaken his head and said, very softly, "I wish I had better news."

So she supposes, if she really has to play that gratitude game, that she's glad the diagnosis has circled her around to Elliott. That part does seem meant to be. When she called the realty company and found herself sobbing "I just want to come home," not even knowing what such a request could mean, the woman on the other end of the line had said they had a cottage that had just come up for rent. Rent with an option to buy.

"Rent to buy is perfect because you don't have to commit all at once," the realtor had said, but somehow Josie had known in that instant, before the woman could even describe the house or give an address, that it was where she was meant to be. The fact that there was only one available had felt like a sign. The second miracle she'd been granted within the narrow span of six months, and while it might have been careless to sign the contract on a place sight unseen, during the whole drive down, following the red lights of the moving truck through the rain, she'd never for once doubted she was doing the right thing. She'd been crying with relief as she'd come through the door last night and who cares if the floor is gritty and the doorframes are wobbly and the appliances are, to use a realtor's word, "temperamental"? She's gotten a bit gritty and wobbly and temperamental herself through the years, so this little cottage suits her, even if whoever had called the place "furnished" was playing fast and loose with the definition of furniture. Even if the view's not remotely what was promised. Prefab shit stacked on stilts cut into the vista, dark and ominous enough that they remind her of those long-legged robotic tanks in a Star Wars movie. But the water's the same as she remembers, and the smell of the air.

She's tired. She barely slept last night and the sun always makes her sleepy so even though she's only unpacked a few boxes, maybe no more than six out of twenty, Josie sits down on the couch and listens while the soft-voiced man tells his nervous student that she needs to stand back from her canvas.

Take a moment, he says. Stop and stand back. That's really the only way to see the picture before you as a whole. To understand when you've let some things get too big and kept others small and failed to grasp that elusive thing called perspective. Losing perspective, the man gently tells his student -dropping his voice so low that it feels like he's shouting- is such an easy thing to do.

"True that," Josie says to the television. She wishes she had another beer. She'd only brought six down from Charlotte and she drank five last night and one on the beach this morning. But even so, it would seem that the occasion calls for a toast. She gets up and adds Michelob and mayo and coffee filters to her grocery list and considers the fact that not a single person from her old life knows exactly where she is right now. Her

60

kids are going to think she's crazy for fleeing to the coast when she still has four follow up post-chemo appointments back in Charlotte every other Tuesday and they're going to say things like "Did you have to go to the beach of all places, Mom, and did you have to go this particular week? Why did you sign a lease? Now you're going to be stuck on Elliott through the fall when the crowds leave and the restaurants close and it's creepy and there's nothing to do. Won't you get lonely? What if -and it won't of course- but what if the cancer comes back? What if you slip and hit your head on the edge of the tub or it's an especially bad season for storms or one of those drifter guys you're always seeing on the true crime shows starts casing empty houses during the off-season? What if he realizes there's a single woman -old, sick- hunkered in all by herself down in the dunes? What happens then?"

Life is all about timing, they'll tell her. And the timing for this particular move...well anybody thinking clearly would tell you. It just isn't right.

Josie looks at the phone hanging on the wall in front of her. Cell service is so bad on the beach that people generally keep a land line, even now, and she walks over and pulls the receiver from its cradle and says "hello," even though she knows perfectly well that it's dead. But she can get it hooked back up, she thinks, and it probably still works, with a little help, and the kids...God, she loves them, more than anything, but her kids are going to just have to let go and hush up and it would seem that poor painting lady on the TV must have gotten herself some perspective because now she's wailing. She pulls her bad painting off the easel and throws it to the floor. The whole thing is too bad to salvage.

Unredeemable. That's what she says.

Her reaction has to be staged. Nobody really throws things to the ground and cries out big words like "unredeemable." The soft-voiced man on TV bends and picks up the woman's painting and tells her that nothing is too bad to be salvaged. You just have to be willing to retrace your steps a bit. Figure out exactly where it was that you first went wrong.

"Sure, 'cause that's a snap," Josie mutters to the screen but the painting teacher has put

the unredeemable picture back on the easel
and is explaining that where we think we
messed up is hardly ever where we really
did. Odds are the real problem was born a
brushstroke or two before and it just takes
us a moment to see it.

"We do not suffer in the moment of our
mistake," the man whispers. "The suffering
comes much later, when we realize our
mistake." Which is probably true but Josie's
had so much truth lately that it's making her
head hurt and now that she's had time to
consider it she's decided that the beige wall
in front of her, the one with nothing but a
phone and a 1996 tide chart, is some sort of
challenge. There are cans of house paint out
under the porch. She saw that much last
night when she drove up with those
wretched half-assed teenagers she hired to
move her from Charlotte. She saw the cans
and thought that some nice person must
have taken a stab at freshening the place up
before they put it on the market. It's
probably outdoor paint, not designed for a
kitchen wall, but then Josie can't quite think
why there'd be any difference between
exterior walls and interior. A wall's a wall
and it seems like either kind of paint should

work okay and besides, she's the one who's here now. This is her house, she reminds herself. At least for the next six months.

And so Josie walks outside, flinching in the brightness of the slanted afternoon sun, and gets down on her knees to reach towards the three cans hiding under the porch.

There's a sort of medium blue, nothing special, then another can of pale green and a soft cream-curdled yellow. What do they call that? She squints at the label. OK, Cornflower. Three colors that don't appear anywhere on the house, inside or out, so she must have been wrong about a nameless kind soul trying to prepare this place for her. There's no telling how long this paint has been here, slowly drying out under the porch, but she still lies belly down beneath the steps and stretches out until she can give each can a good yank. Pull them loose from their nesting place and drag them into the light. The pale blue is called April Morning, the soft green is Seafoam and she wonders what would it feel like to have every wall in the living room a different color. Well, maybe two of them Cornflower, since that's the heaviest can. It's probably a waste of time because she can't imagine that she'll ever have visitors, at least not until Labor Day when her family will no doubt appear en masse to drag her out the door and force her to face what they call reality.

Josie rocks back on her heels and teeters there like a bad yogi, considering how a woman might begin to make a whole life out of April Morning and Seafoam and Cornflower. She knows she's not an artist. She's not even one of those wannabes they find to put on painting shows. But, at least from now until the end of December, she owns these walls and she owns this paint and there's nobody around to stop her from trying to live her own life.

****

Cully knows she shouldn't have started carrying on about poison cocktails and hearts that keep beating after you're dead. She scared the young people right off. Eventually she even lost Josie.

Cully raises a dark, wrinkled hand to her brow and looks down the beach. It's starting to empty a bit although the dog walkers and the shell seekers will be back soon enough. Her unsteady eyes settle on the lone figure of a man. Pot-bellied, stooped, but still moving well enough. One might even say moving admirably well, considering that he seems to be her age or better. There's something about that slope in his shoulders and the way he looks down when he walks that reminds her of someone she knew long ago, in her own girlhood.

Cully's not normally sentimental. She's not one to think about bridges burned and roads not taken or to save ticket stubs and pressed flowers. People who know her always say that the ability to face hard facts and move on is her finest quality but something feels different about this summer. She's caught herself drifting into the past more and more, as if memory carries more joy than anticipation, and she wipes her eyes and stares again, this time harder.

It's pointless. The man grows even more blurry. Everything is, the way the world looks when you have sunscreen in your eyes.

Only Cully didn't rub on sunscreen this morning before she came out. She gave up on preventative measures years ago. So what if the collection of brown splotches spilling across her chest is beginning to look more and more like a map of the Caribbean? Her doctor scolds her for her tan -so unfashionable these days, the equivalent of smoking or driving without a seatbelt, and Cully knows he's right. She's managed to live her way into a more cautious time. It's like the whole world has sobered up from a long drinking binge and she might turn cautious too, if she had anything left to lose. But the chemicals in sunscreen make her chest feel tight and itchy and being vigilant just doesn't seem worth it anymore. There comes a point in every woman's life when she realizes that the cure is worse than the disease.

Cully's phone vibrates and she glances down, even though she knows the only people apt to be sending her a message work at either AARP or CNN. Her swimsuit is old, stretched out, faded, and she can't remember how long she's had it. It's hard to find a swimsuit actually made for swimming anymore. But now that her breasts have parted ways and taken off for territories unknown, the bra has become two handy pockets for phones and keys. Today for some reason Cully kept noticing the bodies of the younger women. Clio's chest still standing up there high and proud, all but saluting the flag, and Amy...well she's been slowed down a bit by having three kids, and once a woman's carried twins none of her parts ever spring back completely, so Amy's having to reckon with some spread in her hips and thighs. Sorting out a bit of sag beneath the armpits, a very slight fold above her belly button, but still. Her body is beautiful and strong and whole and it made Cully sad to see what pains Amy took to hide herself. She'd walked out with the sleeves of a man's shirt tied low around her hips and one of those bathing suits with the tummy panels built in. All morning Amy had kept looking at Clio, bending and twisting in that unself-conscious way of the very young, with envy on her face. Cully had wanted to say "you're beautiful too," but then she decided not to waste her breath.

Women never seem to appreciate the glory of their own bodies and there's no point in trying to convince them. They keep paddling around the warm sea of youth, carrying on about silly things, imagining there's a difference between being thirty-six and twenty-two when really, there isn't. Young is young. It's only old that has degrees. Women like Clio and Amy don't understand yet that every birthday past the age of forty includes a thief on the guest list. That he waltzes into the party unashamed, blending in with your friends and family, acting like he has every right to be there, but then, just when you least expect it, he takes something from you. You don't even know that anything's missing for a while but then, at some point weeks or months down the road, you go to get it and you realize this thing you're reaching for, this thing you've spent a lifetime taking for granted, is suddenly gone. It might be your titties, the fourth vertebra of your lower back, your grip strength or maybe it's just your ability to remember the capitals of South America or to clip your own toenails or hoist the cast iron stock pot from the lowest shelf or sleep or shit or fuck. But the day comes when, just like that, you look up and notice for the first time that somehow these things are gone.

Stolen. Taken from you maybe years ago, back at some point when you were too careless to notice.

How long has it been since a man has touched her? Cully isn't thinking about sex. That ship has not only sailed, it's hit an iceberg and sunk. Cully knows that a young woman, someone like Clio with her pretty boys and her porch shower and twenty-dollar tips from the tables full of golfers, would never believe how easy it will be to live without sex someday. How it actually feels good to walk the world free of men with your arms swinging back and forth unencumbered. No, this isn't about sex-Cully's just trying to remember what it means to be touched. There was a time when her skin was hungry. When she wasn't so brave and solitary and pure. A time when she knew how to fold into things. Make herself soft and small. Slip inside the envelope of a man and let him lick her and stamp her and send her someplace new.

The man in the distance turns to throw something into the water and then stands, waiting patiently, for the waves to bring it back to him. Cully keeps her cupped hands to her brow and is dimly aware that she's been holding her breath, all this time.

It does look like him. But it can't be. The man she's thinking of left this world years ago.


\*\*\*\*


"He's so cute," Jeannie says.

Clio looks up from cutting lemons. The pile of orange wedges are already cleaned and sliced and stacked neatly in a corner of the cutting board. The cherries are the messiest so she leaves them for last. "You say that every day."

"He's cute everyday," Jeannie says. "Oh, c'mon Cli-baby, you know he looks all the world like Jack Kennedy."

"Not so much," Clio says, unwilling to give the girl the satisfaction. You have to be careful with someone as needy as Jeannie. You tell her anything, you show her the least little sliver of sisterhood, you say "me too" about the smallest of observations like yeah, it's hot or yeah, my back hurts, and then she up and decides the two of you must be best friends. Starts writing "sisters" on the back of snapshots and buying birthday gifts and calling you up when she's drunk at midnight and shit like that.

"He does too," says Jeannie. She's pulled up a barstool and stationed herself directly across from Clio, as if they're about to deal a round of cards. She's evidently set all the tables and laid out the silverware and yet she makes no move to help Clio with her own tasks. Instead, she props her chin on her hands and swivels her body toward the heir to the Spanish Moss- hell, the heir to half of Elliott Point if the gossips are to be believed.

He feels the girl's stare. How could he not? Jeannie could bore through walls when she gets focused on something and so after a second or two Jack looks up and grins at both of them, the sort of smile that shows off the best that American orthodonture has to offer. Clio, who's always been self-conscious about the slight protrusion of her front teeth, looks down reflexively but Jeannie beams back, gaps and all. Jack and his dad have spread what looks like an architectural blueprint across one of the wooden tables and through the glass window behind them, this rich boy and his hard-ass father, Clio can see Dupree out in the gravel parking lot, starting to unload his truck. He's standing up in the flatbed, bare-chested, a wooden crate of tomatoes precariously balanced on his shoulder.

Jeannie follows her gaze." And that one, he looks like..."

"James Dean."

"James Dean?"

"You know, that dead movie star. At least that's what popped into my mind earlier today."

"All right then," says Jeannie, her voice showing she's not totally in agreement. But she seems to like the symmetry of the names because after a second or two of mulling it over, she nods vigorously. "James and Jack," she says. "The farm boy and the frat boy. Both of them perfect in two different ways and both of them absolutely batshit crazy about you. Here I can't get even one man to give me a whirl and you have the two hottest guys on the beach lining up to take their chance. I guess that's what life is like when you're pretty."

Clio starts to say "not so much" again but there's really no point in arguing on this one. She's pretty and everybody knows it. Physical beauty is the only thing life gave her right out of the gate, maybe as sort of an apology for all the other things she didn't get. Like some angel with a cracked-ass sense of humor stepped forward and said "Okay, so your mama'll be on the steps of the church every time the doors are opened, holding a mushroom soup casserole and yammering about visions of Jesus. But then when Friday and Saturday roll around the church doors will close and the bottle will open and for the next forty-eight hours she won't be worth a shit. And your daddy'll be charming in the way of one of those southern scholars who leans on his hoe and says smart stuff about Faulkner and the solar system, but then when your mama opens the bottle, he'll turn away from all his philosophy and sniff the air and from that point on he won't be worth a shit either. And somehow all the church-going and the book-learning will make it worse. It'll show you what they could have been and in the end that'll be what breaks your heart. The squandering of their possibility. Your folks might've been fine people, exceptional even, and sometimes, for a bit here and there, they are. But most of the time you'll be left on your own to grow up in a ten-unit trailer park at the end of a rutted road. Lonely and scared and just living for the day the bookmobile comes. But wipe your eyes, little girl, because here, looky here. The same angels who took your mama and daddy's good sense have decided to bend down and give you a little parting gift. Be sure to pick up a headful of naturally blonde hair and wide green eyes and a straight nose and big tits on a skinny body as you exit. And thank you very kindly for playing."

"Pretty isn't everything," Clio says, standing there with cherry juice on her hands, the color brighter than blood, and just as apt to stain. Her eyes are still fixed on the window. Or maybe she's really looking at the table in front of it.

Jeannie has started spinning on the stool, slapping the side of the bar each time she passes, giving herself just enough of a shove

75

to keep the game going. Most of the time she acts more like she's nine than nineteen. "Pretty ain't everything. Yeah. So says the girl who's got James Dean and Jack Kennedy, both of them eating out of the palm of her hand."

\*\*\*\*

*Josie's right. It's looking more and more like she's not going to marry him,* Cully thinks. *Even though we all know she probably should. But she's a stubborn little cuss and she seems determined to find a way to make it work with the rich one. She thinks money will make her life easy.*

*Which it will.*

*For a while.*

\*\*\*\*

This is not a voice that she's heard before. Amy's sure of at least that much. But the whispering...that little-girl, baby-talk crap. It's too over the top, obviously fake. So maybe she really has heard this voice before, just not like this.

Think, Amy, think.

If her husband, never a bold man, somehow out of nowhere got bold enough to take himself a mistress, who would it be? From early October through late March, Elliott Point is a sleepy little outpost. The perfect place for a tryst, should a man be the trysting kind, but then comes this time of year when you've got summer people everywhere, washing in and out with the tide. Their very numbers create a diversion and Amy supposes if a man wanted to betray his wife and risk his family -especially a man who was rich enough, still handsome enough, who had that intoxicating whiff of small town power...

So that's no help. There's no telling who this woman might be, local or tourist, or when the whole thing might have started, so Amy has to come at this another way, enter the house of betrayal through another door. If a man was having an affair, who would know about it? His golfing buddies? The businessmen on the town council? Rotary Club? Zoning council? Volunteer Fire Department? Men stick together. Even if those men she socializes with, the husbands of her girlfriends, the guys she rarely thinks about nine months of the year but still counts as summer friends...even if they knew, they wouldn't tell her. They'd just look at her with pity.

Would they tell their wives?

Now there's a thought. For months, going on years, she might have been the laughing stock of the whole yacht club. Yacht club. The sign on the dock is another ridiculous affectation because the Elliott Point basin doesn't have anything remotely approaching a yacht, only a handful of speedboats and pontoons. Hell, the sign pointing you off the main road's bigger than the dock when you get there and Amy's always considered herself the clear headed one of their social circle. Less materialistic, more pragmatic, able to see through the leather-seated golf carts and Chivas Regal and Hermes scarves. Able to call it all out, at least in her own head, as the bullshit it surely is. Nothing more than the desperate accoutrements of a bunch of country people come to town.

But maybe she's been the butt of the joke all along, without even realizing it.

No. No. Sinking into that kind of self pity won't help her. She's got to come at this yet another way. It doesn't matter when it started or who knows about it. If Brian really is slipping away with a strange woman, where would they meet to do it? Affairs don't float in thin air. Sex has to happen in some actual place.

Certainly not in his Beamer. No normal sized woman could stretch across those tiny bucket seats and they probably didn't do it on the beach either. Her husband is finicky. He has a thing about sand spurs and October flies and he sure as shooting can't check into a hotel. Everyone in town knows him. Does this woman have a house, an apartment or condo? Would he dare to go there, to risk being seen slipping inside an inappropriate door?

Or...Amy looks up to the landing and takes it all in. The expansive ceilings above her, the paired sets of curved stairs leading to the children's rooms beyond. The open catwalks climbing even higher, climbing to a view of the stars, and then there's the matter of the grand entry from the road, the one she insisted on, with its wrought iron gate and curved brick wall, perfect for hiding a stranger's car.

He wouldn't do it here, would he? There's no way he would bring his winter woman into their summer house.

But the minute Amy thinks the thought she knows that's exactly what must have happened. She and the kids didn't come down until the middle of June this year. Right after school was out Adam heard he'd made All Stars and that knocked the start of summer back two solid weeks. Merry hadn't liked it. "Daddy's been on Elliott since March," she'd wailed, and that was true—when the building had picked up in the spring Brian had headed straight down to supervise the building project. Sure, he'd tried to make it back to Charlotte for most of the baseball games, and Merry's spring recital, all the stuff like that. Such a good father. Putting so many miles on the road between Elliott Point and Charlotte, trying to see his kids do their stuff while building them up a tidy fortune to inherit, all at the same time.

But any way you care to count them, the numbers add up to days and weeks throughout the spring and into the summer when a man found himself living alone in a sprawling beach home with his family three hours away. Batching, that's what he'd called it. Claimed he'd be batching it from March to June. Eating takeout and watching TV at night and being lonely, just counting the days until his family could join him.

That's what he told Amy. Hell, that's what he told everybody.

But maybe, at the same time...maybe he'd been bringing some woman here. Holding her elbow as she walked up the grand curved steps to Amy's house.

There's no other answer. Nothing else makes sense.

Amy's heart is pounding as she sprints across the landing and jerks open the doors to the master suite. Was the deed done on her very bed, or did he carry the woman out to the deck? There are chaise lounges there.

They'll work as a makeshift bed in a pinch, if a couple gets the urge to feel the breeze on their butts and hear the sounds of the surf in the distance. Brian and Amy used to do just that, in the earlier, happier days of their marriage when the kids weren't as likely to roam around the house all hours of the day and night. Maybe Brian and this woman did both, Amy thinks, feeling queasy. Maybe they made love on this very bed and then took glasses of wine out to the patio. Pushed the lounge chairs together and lay down and looked at her stars and then did it all over again.

Because now that she's had a moment to think about it, she's decided that she must have been victim to an even worse betrayal. Brian and his nameless lover had done more in her house than have sex. They had lived in it. Cooked and drank and read and showered and argued and slept. Hadn't she complained that things were out of place when she finally dragged the kids down the middle of June? Chairs angled a funny way and juice glasses on the wrong shelf. Five ceramic coffee cups dangling on a mug stand designed for six.

Brian had blamed the cleaning service. They banged through each week like a herd of cattle, that's what he'd said, and the changes had been so subtle, so seemingly harmless, that Amy had somehow managed to notice them and ignore them all at once. The alterations she'd found had been slight, as subtle as the movement of a planet around the sun or a retreating tide pulling sand from beneath a woman's feet. So she'd told herself that he must be right and she must be wrong but then there had been the matter of her green silk robe. She was so sure she'd left it here at the end of last summer, but when she'd arrived a couple of weeks ago it wasn't on its normal hook behind the bathroom door. After searching for a while, she'd finally decided that she must be confused, that the green robe had been left somewhere in the back of her closet in Charlotte. Because this is what a man can do. He can make a woman collude in her own betrayal. He can make her ashamed for asking questions. Convince her she's delusional for counting coffee cups. He will explain, pity in his voice, that there are logical explanations for every little clue.

It's so easy to ignore what's missing.

Harder to ignore what's there that shouldn't be.

Amy bursts out of the bedroom door and runs downstairs, nearly stumbling on the stairs. Above her she can hear Merry's music, the low droning beeps and blips from the boy's video games. She goes straight to the kitchen and pulls open the cabinet beside the cooktop, the place where she keeps her oils and spices and, sure enough, there it is. A small jar of Moroccan spice blend.

Amy had never bought this. She has no idea what a person might even do with a Moroccan spice blend and she had pulled it out just a few nights ago, held it up to her husband and said "What's this?" He had only shrugged, turned back to his sports channel, but there's no denying that this woman, whoever she is, has had the temerity (and the turmeric) to help herself to everything in the kitchen. She had meandered down the curved stairs wearing a green silk robe, then she had cooked with exotic quasi-African spices in Amy's kitchen, and slept in Amy's bed with Amy's husband. Carried one of her ceramic coffee cups out on the deck the next morning to enjoy Amy's hard-won view and somehow proceeded to drop the cup. In some ways the cup is the most painful detail. A piece in a matching set now lost because this woman has been careless. She has let Amy's life break left and right.

With her hands trembling, Amy opens the jar of spice and takes a deep long sniff. It's the sort of smell you remember. The sort of smell you yearn for after life has taken it away. Dark. Pungent. Overwhelming. It is the smell of slow but inevitable endings and all at once Amy knows who the woman is who has moved into her house and lived her life. She walks through the open French doors onto the deck, moving straight toward the open blue water and tries to calm her breathing. The dunes feel infinite, the water and the sky even more so. Amy leans back and throws the jar of Moroccan spices as hard as she can. She wails. A banshee scream, loud enough that she even startles herself.

Her son, her oldest, her Adam -born eleven minutes before his sweet brother- did not get his baseball skills from his father. No, his Mama may well be getting ready to risk everything she has in this world, including her sanity, but she still has her throwing arm. The small glass jar sails over the railing and Amy can hear it fall, with a soft thud, into the sand. She imagines watching it roll and sink and finally nestle into the dunes.

"I'm going out on an errand," she yells through the open doors, even though she knows the kids are far above her and lost in their own worlds.

She goes halfway up the steps and tries again, this time yelling louder.

"Merry, you hear me? You're the one in charge. Keep an eye on your brothers. I won't be gone long."

****

The man has disappeared. Gone into the dunes, most likely, cut his way back to the sidewalk that flanks Elliott Point's only real road. Or more likely he never existed in the first place so his disappearance is the most logical thing about him.

Cully sits back in her chair, alone again. The younger ones don't come and sit with her every day. They're busy and Cully isn't. That's pretty much the long and short of it. She's at the point in life where every conversation is a privilege. And yet if she were to be honest, on those occasions when the other three have deigned to spend the afternoon with her they often leave her just like this. Jangled. Restless. Tossed to and fro by their various predicaments. Younger women may find themselves annoyed by older women but they'd be even more annoyed if they knew how often they make those older women sad. Cully often finds herself so worried about their problems that she almost forgets her mantra: that a woman's first and truest calling is to fully live her own life. To sit in the moment, to expand and breathe all the way into every nook and cranny of the day. Cully has sometimes tried to explain to the others that they needn't be so busy. That there is no better use of a woman's time than to sit with this water, these clouds, this unusually slow sunset and this one special tide pull, to stand witness to each perfect and holy cycle of twenty-four hours.

But they don't listen. They can't.

Cully sighs. This is not the way she planned to go into the evening, fretting about three wayward creatures too vain and silly to know the good life even when it slaps them upside the face. Sunset means it's time to make her way slowly over the dunes back to her cottage and her medication, her glass of wine and her Jeopardy! Cully loves Jeopardy! She loves the idea of a game you win by asking questions instead of answering them and in truth she needs her pour of pinot extra bad today. Sometimes memory scrapes her raw and it's good to have something waiting in the fridge to dissolve those sharp edges just a bit. Alcohol makes the darkness ahead seem more soft-focus and tolerable.

She's earned them both today, her Alex and her wine, but the movement of standing up, while slight, is enough to rattle her fragile sense of equilibrium. Cully weaves and then stumbles and her leg brushes against the rusty metal of the beach chair. It stings at once, which means it will only sting worse later, and she drops back down into the chair with an inelegant thud, her heart pounding. Maybe she should rest a few minutes before she tries again. Cully has her good days and her bad ones. This isn't one of the good ones. She'd awakened at five this morning with a nosebleed. A smear of something across her pillow, a funny metallic taste in her mouth. That sound that she hears more and more lately, muffled and repetitive, like the ticking of a clock.

But she'd gotten up anyway -what the hell else is there to do? She'd made her coffee and dragged her chair out here and now she's been sitting all day, lost in the troubles of the other women. Her three girls, she calls them and first it was Clio running out of the porch shower with a towel wrapped around her so loosely that you could see a flash of her butt as she sprinted across the unpainted wooden boards. There had been a small guilty pause, Cully staring and trying not to, and then that one-named boy had come out after her, glancing left then right before he stepped buck naked into the daylight.

It had been a while since Cully enjoyed the full study of a man and this one was the sort statues are made from. Josie had called him "pretty" but Josie, as is her tendency, had gotten the situation half right and half wrong. "Pretty" is such a trivial word and the young couple running across the splintery porch in the first flush of a summer afternoon...they had been practically glistening with vitality and energy and promise and everything that matters. And then there's Amy up there in the distance, standing on her high deck, with her arms folded tight across her chest like somebody's just hit her. Standing like she expects somebody to hit her again.

In some ways, Amy is the one who frets Cully the most because if there were any solid "shoulds" to life, Amy's the one who "should" be happy, living in her fine house with an unfettered view of the world and her kids all three safe and healthy and still close at hand. And yet Amy is by far the most miserable of the lot. It's just like Cully was telling Josie. Amy's busy making the same mistake as a million thousand hundred women before her- she's letting a trifling man pull her down. Maybe she bent over, only thinking she was trying to help him, thinking that stooping to show him kindness was nothing more than the charity of a moment, nothing more. Yet somehow in the process of rescuing men women always seem to be the ones who end up taking the fall. They tumble right over themselves until some magic transference of power occurs and the trifling man is the one standing up and walking away, brushing off the dust and not looking back, and the woman is the one left behind, sprawled on the sand, trying to catch her breath. Wondering how the hell her strong and upright life could have gone so wrong.

Granted, in this particular situation the man in question is Amy's husband. That counts for something, Cully will concede this much. "Husband" is one of the world's big words. Even an artist has to acknowledge the weight of it. Has to stop and bow down a little. Head of the household, breadwinner, father of her children, flesh of her flesh, 'til death do they part. All of which had been true of Cully and her own husband and yet, and yet...

And yet women aren't supposed to say this, but when the day of reckoning finally comes, even the man you called "husband" can become nothing more than a flicker in the sun. Can disappear with amazing speed, leaving very little vestiges of himself behind. At least if he's not the one who took your heart.

Cully closes her eyes and tries to send a message to Amy. To send it telepathically across the dunes. *If your Brian boy has really become all this awful, and we both know he has, then you're just gonna have to pack up your car and your kids and your jar of Duke's mayonnaise and leave his sorry ass.* This is what Cully thinks, even though she knows it's never that easy. Even if she knows the most sorry-ass of all sorry-ass men still have more power than the most sparkling of women and as Cully stares at the house in the dunes and tries to focus, Amy abruptly rears back and throws something. The shock of the gesture, even from this far away, startles Cully and an involuntary cry escapes her lips. It seems that the flying object almost hits Josie, who is next door, in her own ratty excuse of a yard.

Dear God. Josie. Now you'd think at least that one would be old enough to know better but there she is on her hands and knees, pulling something from beneath her steps.

What's to be done with any of them? They are their own worst enemies and now Josie has pulled out a trio of big rusty cans. Cully watches as Josie half-tugs and half-rolls them to the only grassy spot in the yard and gives each metal tub, in turn, a gentle kick. Then she bends and takes something, a screwdriver most likely, and starts trying to pry off the lids.

*Quit that,* Cully wants to holler, even though she knows Josie can no more hear her than Clio and Amy can. *Those are not your colors. They're too soft, they're too nothing, all fading away and polite. Stores sell paint to 59-year-old women, for god's sake. Just go walk yourself up the concrete aisles of a Lowe's and take some of those little strips of color in your hand and for once in your life, choose a shade that's strictly to your own liking. You're worth more than the leftover, half-dried-out remnants of somebody else's dream.*

Cully settles back in her seat. Looks back at the ocean, flat and gray and plain at this point, just one more unpainted canvas. Sometimes she wonders if she is losing her mind. She knows she's slowing down. Almost every day she drops her keys or loses her glasses. Or she does crazy things like leaving the milk out on the counter and putting her phone in the fridge. She has trouble recalling the names of actresses in old movies. *Kathy Bates*, she catches herself saying out loud. *That's Kathy Bates and that luminous little skinny thing beside her is Jessica Lane. No, Lange. Jessica Lange. That's the name.*

But then before she can congratulate herself too much she goes to the grocery on the corner and runs into a woman she's known for the past twenty years. Really knows, not just an image passing through her mind like Kathy Lane, and wouldn't you know it? The woman's fawning all over Cully, saying she owns three of her paintings and has her eye on a fourth. A good solid customer, money in the bank, but for some reason Cully looks right at her and for the life of her can't come up with the woman's name. All there is to do then is laugh and babble something and hope she comes off eccentric, like an artist, instead of demented, like an old beach bat, even though anybody can look at her and tell it's a bit of a toss-up between the two.

So as sunset approaches on this particular afternoon, prettier than most, and landing, according to Josie, square on the first true day of summer, part of Cully is scared she's losing her mind and another part of her is thinking "good riddance," but there's a whole other third part of her, the clear strong brave part, that knows in some ways she's sharper than ever. Memories -true memories, not the kinds of things they ask on Jeopardy! or the names of people who never did matter- come roaring back to her at times with the force of a freight train. The smell of bacon can nearly knock her to her knees, or the chorus of a song some boy hummed in her ear in her youth, or even the first watermelon of the season - still green and not quite there. More promise than fulfillment, but Cully was a country girl once, and she can't resist grabbing a watermelon the minute the first ones appear at a roadside stand, even though she knows it'll be mealy and hard inside. The first of anything is rarely the best.

Cully resolutely puts her palms to the arms of her chair and digs in her heels and gives it her best push. A rough warmth has encircled her leg. This stranger's leg, speckled and bowed but somehow attached to her body. When she looks down and sees blood in the water it takes a moment for it to register as her blood. Her flesh ripped open when she brushed against the metal on the chair earlier, because it takes hardly anything to tear her these days. It's like she's dissolving...like whatever barriers that once stood between her and the rest of the world are giving up the fight and if she waits long enough, just sitting on this beach looking at the water, she'll turn into nothing and everything all at the same time.

They say sharks feed at sunset. That's when the monsters of the ocean are bold enough to venture close to shore in search of their prey. Danger where you least expect it, here in the shallows, just under the surface of the water, and yet Cully can't seem to stop staring at the swirls of red spinning within the pale clear green of the surf. It's beautiful, enough to hypnotize a woman, and after she looks at them for a moment the shakes take over, hard enough that she closes her eyes one more time, thinking that if she doesn't move soon the water may come in so far she's trapped and besides, she's making a big deal over nothing. There are no sharks here. She's barely thigh deep and she'd see their fins and besides, there's no reason she has to leave right this minute. It's not like she has anywhere to go or anybody waiting for her, unless you count Alex Trebek.

This latest injury is just a surface one, far from the worst she's suffered. It stings in the salt water, but so what? Cully blinks back tears and stares out at the uncertain horizon. She's made plenty of mistakes in her life, but she's never been one to confuse a scrape with a wound.

****

Picture this, if you can: Dupree's truck and Jack's convertible, wedged side to side under a half-baked myrtle tree, vying for what appears to be the only piece of shade in the whole state of South Carolina.

Together, they pretty much tell the story of the choice Clio has to make. Jack and James, that's what Jeannie called the two boys who drive these vehicles, which is fair enough. Two different kinds of love, two different kinds of future. It's like her grandma always said: Marry the man and you marry the life. Of course her grandma always uttered those words with regret and by the time she's an old woman, Clio doesn't intend to have any regrets.

Which isn't to say she knows exactly what she should do next.

The sports car parked under the myrtle may as well have dropped from Mars. Every time Clio climbs into it, she's never sure where to put her hands and feet. It feels strange to be that low to the ground and when Jack pulls his big engine up to a light all the people idling around them take notice, sometimes staring down right into their laps, and Clio starts having crazy thoughts. How any one of those trucks or even a regular sized car could run right over the top of them. How she could be decapitated, just like Marie Antoinette, another girl who married above her raising and lived (not long) to regret it. She imagines that the other people at the light hate her and Jack, the way he plays the radio too loud, not caring a whit who's forced to accept his choice of music, and then there's the matter of his narrow sunglasses, her long tan legs, the way they rip out of there the minute the light turns green. No wonder the common people might be tempted to rise in revolt against them. This is the kind of car that could make a girl lose her head.

But the truck beside it feels familiar. It doesn't take any imagination at all for Clio to envision it bouncing down the same dirt road that raised her, passing the little green farmhouse where her grandma taught her how to make biscuits and quote the beatitudes and make a decent prom dress out of somebody else's Goodwill tax write-off. She's already told Jack some cockamamie story about her parents relocating down to the coast themselves next year, maybe after her daddy retires. As if a man can retire from being a drunk. But the key thing is that Jack can never, never, no not ever see the trailer where Clio grew up and just in case she ever stood a chance of forgetting how ugly that part of Carolina is, life reminded her just a couple of weeks ago when she was driving back from her daddy's birthday. Rushing, trying to make it before the happy hour clock in. There's only a couple of pitiful towns between Dillon and the beach and otherwise nothing but red-dirt fields. If a girl has to pee -and the minute even Clio thinks the question "Do I have to pee?" well then boom, she has to pee- all there is to do is follow some tractor tracks off the road, pull down your shorts and pray like hell that you don't get caught crouched in the dirt with your ass hanging out.

So Clio had found herself a sandy red path that seemed to lead to nowhere and squatted, panties stretched between her ankles and her head whipping back and forth because you never can tell when somebody's going to waltz right out of a corn field. Cotton and tobacco at least let you see trouble coming. But the only things in sight were a couple of shuttered shacks in the distance and a dog, his ribs visible and his eyes wary. She didn't think he was feral but the minute she saw him pushing his head through the stalks, she pulled up her pants even though she was still dripping. Jumped back in the car, panicking for a second when her tires spun, but in a second or two she caught something solid and broke free, pulling back into the pavement without looking left or right, accelerating and reaching for the knob of her radio before she had a chance to get stuck in the past.

Because that's her biggest fear, you know. Getting stuck in the past.

Dupree is standing outside the door that leads to the manager's office, probably waiting to get paid. He tries to catch her eye but Clio turns back to her prep and feigns a profound and sudden interest in a can of pineapple chunks. He lets it go. He might hang around the bar for an hour or so when he finishes -Jeannie's been known to slip him a free beer- but Clio doesn't have to worry about him making a scene. Dupree won't mess it up for her. He's not that kind. He knows that he's her summer boy and she's his summer girl.

And he also knows that, sooner or later, summer always ends.


****



Josie's not actively trying to spy on Amy but it's almost like she can't help it. A minute ago a phone rang. Josie's first thought was that it had come from her own house, which was silly. Her line isn't in yet and even if it was, nobody knows how to find her here. That shrill persistent cry for attention must've been coming from Amy's house and Josie tried to stay focused, even though ignoring a ringing phone goes against every mama-bone in her body.

A minute later something had whizzed by overhead. Sharper and faster than a bird. Somebody must have thrown something, most likely off one of the seven thousand decks of Amy's house, which makes no sense even though Josie knows Amy is unhappy. She knows it's the kind of unhappiness women dare not speak aloud because it seems so ungrateful to complain when you have so much. Bitching in the lap of plenty makes a girl seem greedy and the one thing a good woman knows is that she's not allowed to be greedy. We're the gender that says we're full when we're not. We roll our eyes and say "no more," and let the serving dish pass us by even if we're wild with appetite and for a woman like Amy, who seems to have it all and then some, she knows that trying to express some sort of vague and pointless discontent is to risk the wrath of everyone about her.

And yet...

Okay, so maybe her house looks like a Ralph Lauren catalog blew up. Maybe she's got three kids so cute that they may as well be in a laundry detergent ad and more money than the rest of them rolled together and doubled. None of that changes the fact her husband doesn't pay her any attention. All the Charleston shutters and overstuffed couches in the world can't fix that kind of hurt. And her kids most likely don't care that she's unhappy. It's not a child's job to care if his mother is happy. He wants her to stand still, to stay stuck, to hold his trash when he hands it to her. How old were her children when they stopped handing her their empty juice boxes and candy wrappers, just expecting her to know what to do with somebody else's mess? Josie can't quite remember but she thinks it was when they were in their twenties.

The trouble with being a woman is that women are supposed to know everything. One time, long ago, Josie's husband -good riddance to that bad rubbish- started to go out the door with the stroller and their firstborn, not two days from the hospital, and he'd turned to her and asked "Is it going to rain?" She'd wanted to say "How the hell am I supposed to know? Am I God or some kind of meteorologist?" She hadn't known any more about how the world worked than she had the week before, when she was merely pregnant and not yet a mother, but it would seem that everything was different now. That she'd died a little in childbirth, like all women do, and been reborn as a creature who's supposed to magically know when it's going to rain. A creature who whips around whenever a strange child in the grocery yells "mama," whose blouse floods with breast milk whenever a commercial comes on about starving children in Africa, a woman who feels guilty the moment she hears a phone ring, even though she knows the call can't possibly be for her.

Josie stands up, stretches her aching back. The cry of a phone, a painful cry, the thud of something being thrown from a high deck and now the final series of sounds. She isn't trying to eavesdrop, she really isn't, but living so close that their lives are practically intertwined, how is Josie supposed to avoid the truth? The next thing she hears is Amy calling out something to her kids and pitter-patting her way down the long arc of steps leading to her oyster shell driveway. A car door slams. An engine cranks. She doesn't exactly pull out with a screech of tires -Josie isn't sure the tires of a minivan can even screech- but Amy's definitely leaving with an exclamation point. No pause at the end of the driveway. Just a sharp right turn, dangerous this time of year with all the tourists driving around.

So someone must have called Amy, must've told her something that made her mad and now she's gone off half-cocked thinking she needs to take care of business. Nothing about this is going to end well. Josie stretches again, putting more muscle into it, and looks down at the cans of paint. Sure, they're dried up, but maybe a splash of turpentine can revive them. Turn them liquid again, coax them back into the world of the living and help them remember what color they were once meant to be. She'll paint the porch railing first, she decides, and then she'll walk into town and call her kids from a payphone. Call one and then the other, either in chronological order or alphabetical order or maybe just in order of how likely she thinks they are to forgive her for running off down here half-cocked and trying to start over. For wanting more from her remaining years, be they two or twenty or who knows? Today, out of nowhere, came the thought that maybe she'll have plenty more.

\*\*\*\*

Friday always brings a wave of people right at five, the minute the door opens. Mostly the very young, coming for the happy hour beer, or the very old, looking for their sundown senior specials. It's easy to get them settled. All a girl has to do is get some suds or sweet tea and some hush-puppies in front of them and then leave them be, happy enough, staring out the window at the marsh and taking slow meditative sips. This is usually the point where Clio takes a bit of a break herself. A pause between the prep and the slam, but today she's in no hurry. Last night, just before closing, Jack had sidled up and asked her if she wanted to have a drink with him on her break. He'd whispered it, glancing around as he did so, so the offer must mean something. She's been trying hard not to think all day, but the truth is she's barreling down on a crossroads and there's no use in pretending otherwise.

Clio walks to her own car, a big old Lincoln, given to her courtesy of one of her daddy's drinking fits. Liquor temporarily makes him nicer and she'd taken off in the thing before he'd had a chance to sober up and change his mind, even though the car's as clumsy as a boat and she's always joked that you dock it more than you park it. She pulls open the door, wincing at the heat coming off the chrome handle, and punches open the glove compartment. Pushes the button that pops the trunk and takes out the only thing she owns of any value. A camera she bought two years ago. Second-hand, but it's a Nikon. The real thing, solid and valuable. When she looks through the lens she has the fleeting impression that she can see the world clearly, at least for a moment.

Focus. That may be the most beautiful word in the English language, and Clio knows she must focus now. Jack and Dupree are both just a few yards away, biding their time in that cinder block building. Both of them wanting to give her something and both wanting to take something away and this is what she must think about, if what she gets is the equal or better of whatever she's being asked to leave behind. There's a harshness to these calculations and yet she must make them. It may just be the first day of summer but still –in all the ways that matter, time is running out.

"So what you gonna do?"

Clio jumps. She didn't sense Jeannie coming up behind her, didn't even hear the crunch of her sneakers through the gravel of the parking lot, which is proof of how distracted she's become. Clio whirls around, faces the girl who she knows both wants to be her and sort of hates her, and takes note of the fact Jeannie has somehow gotten a big stain of the red cherry juice right in the middle of her apron. It looks like she's been stabbed and hasn't even noticed.

"Right now I'm going to take a picture."

"Of what?"

"Of these two cars. Sitting under this crepe myrtle tree."

"Why?"

"So I won't forget them. Won't forget this day."

Jeannie frowns. "Nobody can forget their own life."

This is such a stupid comment that Clio doesn't even bother responding. She looks through the viewfinder and clicks, and then steps back and sighs, because, sure as shooting, here they come. Three carloads full of church ladies, pulling in at the same time they do every day, about twenty minutes after the construction boys chasing their one-fifty beer. Most of the church ladies' husbands are dead, and even if they aren't, no woman wants to fry her own fish. It stinks up the kitchen and with so many seafood shacks crowding the point, the flounder so cheap and plentiful, you'd be a fool not to grab a bunch of your girlfriends and catch the senior special. Clio knows she'll be stuck with this table, like she generally is. Jeanne's already got her eye on another carload pulling in, this one full of men, flushed and mottled from a day on the links. Ordering the first round before they're even seated or maybe they've already started drinking, who can tell?

Either way they'll give a girl a Jackson for a bourbon and branch and not say a word about the change. Fifty-year-old men tip well and seventy-year-old women tip crappy so Jeannie will find some way to weasel her way toward the golfers, even if Valerie ends up seating them in Clio's section. Never mind. Not to worry. Focus, Clio. The day is swiftly coming where any dead president, be it Washington or Jackson, isn't going to matter to you at all.

"Look at them," she says to Jeannie, jerking her chin toward the door where the old women are filing in, one at a time, each of them holding it open for the walker behind her. "Look at them right in their faces and then you tell me they haven't already forgotten own lives. That's why I take my pictures. I plan to remember it all. The good and the bad."

"I don't know why anybody would want to remember this pile of shit," Jeannie says. "God, girl. I love you like a sister, but you're damn weird." She pauses for a long moment and when she finally speaks there's something like triumph in her voice. "Now here's something for your photo album," she says. "Look who's coming out the door. I swear if it ain't both of them."


****


The minute you cross the bridge, the world changes.

Amy has thought this exact same thought each time she's driven over the little swing bridge that marks the line between the island and the real world.

The bridge is the symbol of Elliott. It was built in 1932 and they put it on shot glasses and t-shirts in the bargain stores, but nostalgic or not, it makes the transition from the mainland to the beach a slow process. Water trumps land down here. Always has, so cars are forced to stop whenever a boat's passing. Barriers drop shakily into place while the bridge unhinges and visitors, having made the godawful interstate trek

111

from Ohio or Pennsylvania, most often take the break as an excuse to roll down their windows. For a moment they inhale the salty breeze coming off the marsh, and they maybe call out something to their kids in the back about looking at the boat. "It's a shrimp trawler," they say, even though it may or may not be. Yankees think everything is a shrimp trawler.

But no matter. Waiting to be allowed entrance into summer is a time-honored Elliott ritual and, no matter who you are or how far you've come, watching the bridge slowly yawn open feels like the start of something. Maybe just a week of vacation or maybe something far more magical, because this particular beach has certain powers. Amy's always known that. It may just be a little slip of a barrier island, with the ocean on one side and the marsh on the other and no more than a hundred houses nestled in the dunes between, but there's a spirit to the place. No matter what she's just been through, the waters of Elliott can wash a woman clean.

"We're going have to do better." That's what Brian says. "If we're going to turn this island into a true destination, then we need to build one of those big vaulting bridges with room for the boats to go underneath. That way nobody will have to stop."

"People like to stop," Amy told him. "You can't think unless you stop."

"People don't like to think."

"Are you sure? Maybe they like to be held up for a minute so that they're kind of forced to say to themselves 'Winter's over. I've made it. I'm here.'"

The two of them had been sitting on the deck when they had this conversation. It had been one of those rare mornings where he didn't dash off before breakfast. He'd put his coffee cup down and looked at her strangely. Like he was really seeing her, like for a minute he'd remembered who'd he'd married, and why.

Then he'd said "They might like it the first time. The first time it's a novelty. But the second time they hear that bell clanging and see that bridge disconnecting- let me tell you, the second time they groan and the third time they curse. Because anything that seems charming at first invariably becomes a pain in the ass over time."

Invariably? That's never been one of Brian's words. It's not even normal for him to cuss. Amy's hardly ever heard her husband say "ass" in fifteen years of marriage, not even when both of his hands were gripping hers.

Amy had started to say something that very moment, to accuse him of quoting Joe or Ernie, one of the other boys in the developmental group. She sensed that he'd been listening hard to other people lately because he kept talking about how they had to clean up the gas stations and bargain stores clustered around the entrance to the bridge on the mainland side. Eyesores, he called them. Can't let Elliott fall victim to the kind of low-rent commerce that's cheapened so many other beaches before it. Can't let it turn into just one more Kmart by the Sea.

Ass and eyesores and cheapened. He never used to talk like that.

"Nine minutes," he said, that morning on the deck. He'd held up nine fingers in case she'd somehow managed to misunderstand. "That's how long the average vehicle has to wait if the bridge happens to be open. If you're in a hurry, nine minutes can feel like a lifetime. But if we get ourselves a high vaulted steel bridge, we can cut the commute from crap to paradise down to 53 seconds flat." So now the mainland was "crap." The same mainland where she'd been born. Where he was from too, at least most of the year. The mainland where Brian had insisted on raising their kids.

But the bridge isn't blocked today. No boats are in sight. Amy bounces across it in her minivan, braking for the turn-off. Makes the sharp left and inches down the steep incline to the parking lot at the edge of the water and looks across the marsh toward the construction site. The crew has already broken down that little half-assed retaining wall and a dozen or so pilings have been driven into the marsh. Thirty or forty more to follow. Risky or not, her husband and his friends are determined to build on the unbuildable. To shore up the shore, to turn a scrap of unsteady, suspect land into the most expensive real estate between Wilmington and Charleston.

Amy eases to a stop and jumps out of the minivan. Leaves the keys in it and the windows rolled down. She knows most of the construction guys and they say good afternoon to her as she passes. She is, after all, the boss man's wife.

One of them ventures to tell her Brian isn't there. She nods but keeps walking.

She didn't come here to see Brian.

****

Josie hasn't been completely honest. Not with her friends or her children and especially not with herself.

She tells them she has happily chosen to downsize, which on the surface of things is true enough. The cottage is no more than 900 square feet, which forced her to be rather brutal with her former possessions. She has travelled eastward from Charlotte with one pair of black pants, six drinking glasses, a single lamp, three towels, and four plates. She'd hired a couple of down-on-their-luck foster kids who'd done yard work for a friend of a friend to help her make the move and then, late last night when she unpacked, she realized they'd stolen from her. Her engagement ring -no longer worn, but still somewhat ironically cherished- was gone, along with a couple of pieces of silver that had been left to her by her mother-in-law. And other, odder things. She'd packed a pair of kid leather gloves she'd purchased one time on a trip to New York. Bought them just to wear while she was there and then carried them home to Charlotte to dig out only on those truly cold nights. She'd rarely needed them, rarely had much practical use for such an item, but from the minute she'd laid eyes on them, those gloves had held a strange enchantment for Josie. She'd imagined she could feel the pulsations of the city in her fingertips each time she pulled them on. They were a statement piece - bright red, trimmed in copper thread- even though Josie generally wears black and takes a certain pride in her plainness. But this particular pair of gloves, over time, had come to represent a second life she'd somehow forgotten to live.

*These gloves were always mine*, she would think whenever she put them on. *They were waiting for me to find them in that little shop in Chelsea and buy them without asking the price.* Like most divorced women too proud to take alimony, Josie has spent a lifetime asking the price, but not this time. She had worn them right out of the shop, only imposing on the girl behind the counter to find a pair of scissors and cut the tag holding them together.

She isn't sure why the loss of them wounds so deep. She'll certainly have no need for a pair of red leather gloves living here at the beach and besides, up to this point she had sacrificed so heartlessly, even getting rid of all her Christmas ornaments and childhood pictures of the kids. *Bring only what matters,* she had told herself over and over and yet she still had taken the New York gloves. Packed them in the same box with the silver, which is probably why they were stolen, almost by accident, and she had stood there alone in the house, her one lamp plugged in but sitting on the floor, her one bulb sputtering and struggling to give her hope, and realized the gloves were gone. Along with the ring and the silver and damn, come to think of it, even her CD player.

Her eyes had filled with tears. It would have felt good to let them fall, but it would seem that the ability to break loose and really sob is another thing Josie has lost along the way. She had tried to cry the day the doctor said "Unfortunately yes, a malignancy," and then when she had sat there frowning like some sort of imbecile, he'd thought that she was too stupid to comprehend and had felt compelled to add the worst word in the world.

"Cancer," he'd said. "I wish I had better news, but it's cancer."

She should have wept then. But all she could do in that doctor's office was what she did last night when she realized she'd been robbed: stand very still, stare into space, and try to figure out exactly what it is she was feeling.

Grief comes at you in pieces. There was the matter of the actual operation, of course, and surgery always feels like a violation. She still hasn't been able to take a single bath without looking down at the scar on her chest and each time she thinks the same thing. That her breast has been stolen. Not that she'd lost it -not even the most careless of women could lose part of her own body- but that it had been violently wrested from her chest. Last night, lying on her couch, too tired to put sheets on the mattress, she had tried not to think about the foster kids, those young men she'd told herself she was only trying to help. She'd bought them hamburgers before they'd begun. Super- sized, the works, and they'd thanked her. They had sung and joked as they packed and it didn't take them long. She'd already spent weeks stripping her life down to the bare minimum and at one point the taller boy, the quieter one, had looked over at her and said "This really all you got?"

It had almost been like he was the one feeling sorry for her. That he was thinking here was this woman, grandma aged, far older than his own wayward mama, no longer able to pick up and move her own stuff. Not even the light pieces, not even boxes of towels and pillows. The more Josie thinks about it the more she feels like she deserved to get robbed. It's what she gets for being a fool, for trying to be kind. She hadn't flinched a bit when those kids had looked up from their burgers and asked for the four hundred in cash. She'd paid them up front and they had said thank you. They'd said it shyly, even called her ma'am and held the door as they'd walked out into the McDonald's parking lot. "Such sweet boys," she'd thought. "Nothing more than kids, really." And yet somehow those sweet boys had been able to feel sorry for her and steal from her at the same time.

Because last night she'd arrived at the house, watched them unload their small truck, waved goodbye, walked up the sagging steps, plugged in her one light, ripped open the first box and almost immediately she could see that, little as she'd packed, she actually had arrived with less than she thought.

Josie has always looked for signs. She can't help herself. It's what comes from a childhood spent sitting on a Baptist pew. The belief had been pounded into her that whatever happens must be happening for a reason and that to live your life thoughtlessly is to spit in the face of God. She had pulled open every box, her movements growing jerkier and more frightened with each rip of the masking tape, certainty fading as she yanked the paltry items from each one. "I've been robbed," she said out loud, and the realization of it hit her like a second blow to the heart. She was already exhausted. She'd been up before dawn and it was now past midnight and she flopped back on her couch, the only properly placed piece of furniture in the whole place, and immediately cried out in pain.

She'd fallen on her stack of plates. Broken the top and the bottom one in the process and popped a bruise on her hip that would only get worse over the next twenty-four hours. It was all so fucking unfair. Almost like she'd said to the universe "I don't need much," and the universe had answered back "Damn right."

So the gloves were gone, and the ring, and her breast and the silver, and her CD player -even though dear God but could she use a bit of music. (The boys had taken the machine and left the CDs. Apparently they didn't care for soft rock from the seventies.) And now she'd fallen ass-first on two of her four dinner plates, which meant that apparently in her new life she was only going to be allowed to have one friend at a time to dinner. And even as she was standing there in the shadow of that single low lamp, with the silence stretching wider than any ocean, she realized that those two boys in a van, one tall and quiet, the other shorter and louder, were belting it down the road driving west and drinking beer or smoking weed, laughing at her. Stupid trusting old woman. Sat in a McDonald's and paid them twenty twenties for the privilege of ripping her off.

She dare not tell her children what happened. They already think she's going senile. She mentioned nothing about the theft on the beach today either, not even to Cully after the younger two had scattered. Josie knows she is being punished for something, maybe for having the arrogance to imagine age would give her some sort of wisdom. Some certainty. The right to declare to the universe that she knows what's really hers.

\*\*\*\*

Clio understands without even looking over her shoulder that Jeannie means Jack and Dupree are both on their way out of the Spanish Moss and heading across the parking lot. It seems bad luck that they should converge on her at once, but also kind of inevitable, so she turns around and smiles as if everything was rolling out just the way she planned it. She sure isn't going to give Jeannie the pleasure of watching her melt in the sun.

"Hey there," she says, nodding in the general direction of all that man sweat and aftershave, making it deliberately vague who she's talking to, but the two boys sort the matter out without a word between them. Dupree hops in his flatbed with just a couple of fingertips to heft him and starts slinging crates around, making more noise than it would seem the occasion calls for. Jack walks right up to his convertible, opens the passenger door and says "Ready?"

"Ready for what?"

"For our drink, silly."

"It's not time for my long break."

"I guess it's time for your long break is whenever I say it is," Jack says, which makes him sound like a jerk, and maybe he is, but Jack also has an ease. That quick smile, that way of sliding his words together, like he's living out exactly everything he was meant to be in one breath and making fun it in another. He winks at Jeannie, who's so excited over the drama that she's practically dancing. And Clio wonders, out of nowhere, if Jeannie has ever even been kissed.

"Besides," Jack says. "Our girl here can cover for you until seven, can't you Ginny?" Jeannie nods, even though she must know that this turn of events means that now she's the one who's going to be stuck with the church ladies and all their quarters and dimes. Jack glances at the camera in Clio's hands.

"And maybe snap a couple of shots while you're at it," he says. "Capture the moment," Jeannie is still bobbing and weaving and Clio doesn't want to hand over her camera. The silly girl's liable to drop it in the gravel or get sand up in the parts or cherry juice or something.

"Dupree?" Clio says. "Do you mind taking our picture?"

He doesn't answer but he does jump right back out of the truck, landing light as a cat. Clio hands him the Nikon, their fingers barely brushing in the transfer. He knows what it means to her and he's seen her use it often enough that he doesn't need any instruction. Clio steps back, closer to Jack, who drapes an arm across her shoulders. It won't be a good photograph. They're squinting straight into the sun and her hair's in a ponytail, like it is when she works, and she's got on that awful puffy shirt with the name of the bar stitched into the pocket, and her stupid red sneakers.

But Dupree twists the focus back and forth and points at them and a second later Clio hears a click. Jeannie squeals.

"Your chariot awaits," says Jack, pulling her toward his car. No time even to get the camera back from Dupree, who merely opens the passenger door of Clio's old Lincoln and sets the Nikon carefully inside. She tries to nod, to thank him, but the moment escapes, like they all do. Dupree is back in the truck, Jeannie is walking toward the restaurant,

stopping now and then to spin in circles as if
some invisible man has asked her to waltz.
All there's left for Clio to do is to descend
into the seat of Jack's car, the black leather
hot enough to brand a girl, and then, quick
as thought, they are moving. Driving so fast
that the row of cypress trees lining the
driveway to the Spanish Moss becomes a
blur and a few strands of Clio's hair break
loose from her ponytail. They swirl around
her face and she wipes them out of her eyes
with one hand while the other is clamped
under Jack's palm. Pressed into his
gearstick, which trembles with anticipation
and power.

No, the picture Dupree took won't be worth a
cuss. Any recollection it managed to capture
will bring nothing but pain. But Clio also
knows that she will keep that photograph.
That she'll insist on remembering every
detail of this day, right up to the very end.

****

"Is it you?"

She must have dozed for a minute because she missed the sight of the old man wading toward her in the water. But here he is, hip deep, looking down with a quizzical little smile on his face. Her chair is perched on what's left of the sandbar, with the pools of salt water deepening all around. You can't find the bottom just by looking. People are always stepping off of sandbars and falling, sometimes turning an ankle or even breaking a leg, which surely this man knows. Yet here he stands.

"I wasn't entirely certain it was you," he says and she nods. Most people look the same on the beach, between their sunglasses and big t-shirts and baseball caps pulled low. Cully realizes that her hat is gone. It must have blown off while she napped.

He hesitates. "You do know who you're talking to, don't you?"

"Don't be foolish," Cully says. "You haven't changed a bit." Which isn't true, but it's the most generous type of lie a person can tell.

"I didn't think you still lived here."

"Left for a while. Came back, like people do. Nobody can stay away from Elliott for long. And you?"

"I live down at the yacht club. I'm the-" he pauses, careful to enunciate the word. "I'm their quartermaster."

It's a simple sentence and yet it takes her a moment to process it. "You say you've been living at the yacht club?"

He nods. "I've seen your paintings. Started to buy one once but I-"He breaks off, looks around.

"But you what? What stopped you?" She's a little afraid he's about to say her paintings are too expensive because she certainly thinks they are. It makes her uncomfortable when the gallery owner puts $700 on a canvas she spent merely an afternoon producing, even though she knows that more than an afternoon truly went into that seascape. Even though she knows that about ninety percent of art work is finished before the painter even picks up her brush.

"No," he says. "They're worth more than what you ask but I-" Again he stops.

She can't stand the silence. "You didn't like it?"

He can make her feel insecure, even after all this time. Maybe it's the way he's looking down while she's looking up, but why the hell is she apologizing for the cost of her paintings? They're the best thing about her. Strangers from all over the country will gladly pay $700 just to see the ocean through Cully's eyes.

"Of course I like them," he says. "I said I was about to buy one, didn't I? But my hut-"

"Hut?" she echoes softly, and with that one word she understands it all. The yacht club doesn't have houses. She doesn't know what she was thinking. He must live in that little shingled shack barely hanging on to the end of the pier.

"But I've certainly seen them," he rushes on, talking fast now as if he's eager to change the subject from where he's living and why. "So I was lying just a minute ago when I said I thought you'd moved away. I knew damn well you lived somewhere on this beach but I never would have thought I'd find you here..."

"Sitting in front of a run-down cottage."

He shakes his head. "It's a fine house. Built good. Good in the bones. I meant no disrespect to your domicile. It's just that you...You've gotten sort of famous."

She's not really famous. Maybe famous by Elliott Point standards but not famous famous and besides, even artists who regularly sell their work rarely wind up with real money. She starts to tell him that hell, a check comes now and then but it's mostly a few hundred and of course she's got a little social security...

"I always pictured you in a mansion with a view," he is saying. "Four stories high, at least. Or maybe living in one of the penthouses on the point."

"Well, you know me," she says. "Deep in my heart I've always craved the simple life."

And with that, she's stumbled upon the words to break the spell. The awful awkwardness between them falls away and they both burst into laughter.

"Oh yeah, that's what you've always been after, all right," he says. "The simple life."

"You want something to drink?" she asks. "I've got a bottle of wine open. We could sit on my deck and kill it for old times' sake."

"I'm not supposed to." When she doesn't answer, he shifts his weight and looks down into her face. "It's a heart thing. Not an AA thing."

"What's wrong with your heart?"

"It got old."

"So what? Mine's old too."

"Happens," he says and Cully knows in that instant that he's lying. It's not his heart, it damn sure is an AA thing and she should stop talking right here, right now. She should let him go back to wherever he came from. And yet somehow she can't quite make herself cut him loose. She doesn't want to be alone tonight.

"My damn doctors," she says, "keep trying to tell me that I need slow down."

"You? Slowing down? Now, I have trouble picturing that."

Which is not a particularly witty thing to say, but she chuckles. It feels good to be with him. "Well, if you get zero drinks a day and I only get one, would you like to come sit and watch me drink it? I think I got some iced tea up there. Lemonade. Stuff like that."

"Please," he says. He pulls her to her feet and they cautiously, with him carrying her chair, begin to pick their way through the maze of tidepools and shallows, moving back in the direction of her house.

\*\*\*\*

Walking into town to call her family is a bit of a preemptive strike. Josie wants to get to them before they get to her. Lay out her plan before they can inform her of theirs.

She'll tell the kids to bring the grandkids down for the rest of the summer, that's what she'll tell them. Drop them off and leave them for weeks at a time if need be. Come back and pick them up whenever it suits. No parent will refuse free babysitting, even if the babysitter in question is a little bit unhinged. They'll start to tell her to be sure to be careful, then they'll stop themselves, and the unsaid words will hang in the air like graffiti on a wall.

But in time they'll come to understand that she means for this little cottage to be a new home base for all of them. Sure, summer's the easy part. Summer's what pops in your head when you close your eyes and think "beach," but she's got to make them see that she's not afraid of the winter. That part of her craves the silence and the isolation, the way the wind cuts when it comes off the dark purple water.

They'll understand eventually. Children always do. Eventually.

It's a mile, more or less, to the pier which means another mile back. Josie tries to ignore the heaviness in her chest as she scrambles up the first dune. Sooner or later she's got to get back to exercising and it may as well be today. She's skidding her way down the other side when she sees Cully, walking up from the water with somebody beside her, carrying her chair. Josie doesn't think she's ever seen him and Cully's certainly never mentioned knowing any sort of man. She tends to act like they don't even exist, but there you go. This one looks scruffy, unkempt, almost derelict, but he's probably just another artist, someone Cully knows from the gallery or the guild. It's hard to tell the creative from the mad at first glance and half the time Cully walks around looking like she's homeless herself.

Josie stands stock still in the shadow of the dune and watches the man take Cully's arm as they turn toward the path. He seems to steady her, or maybe she's the one steadying him. It's hard to be sure from this distance, but Josie even thinks Cully may even put her head on the stranger's shoulder, might submit to a quick embrace.

Josie has always hoped that someday somehow she'll turn into Cully- strong, independent, blunt as a crowbar but still known and respected by everybody on the beach. How many winters has the woman spent down here alone? More than Josie can count, but the place hasn't broken her. She's still got her mind and her spirit.

And apparently even a bit of a beau.

****

The man opens her door as if it was his door, as if he was entitled to enter her private spaces at will. Normally Cully would bristle at such masculine presumption, but today's she's got a lot on her mind. Neither one of them speaks for a minute, waiting for their heartbeat to return to normal from the walk.

"Make yourself at home," she mutters under her breath, walking into the kitchen and reaching for the bottle of wine with one hand and the corkscrew with the other. She chooses the good Cabernet, the kind that comes up on fifty a bottle, but it's a special occasion. It's not often that a ghost comes to call.

He's already moved out to her little studio, an add-on room covered in glass. He wanders among her paintings, stopping at first one and then the other. "Didn't think I'd find you here," he says softly, as if talking mostly to himself. "Figured you'd be up in one of those fancypants condos at the point."

"You already said that and you can just bite your tongue," she calls from the kitchen.

"Can you really imagine me paying a king's ransom for a six-inch view of the water?"

"They pick up your trash, you know."

"Your trash?"

"Yep. All you have to do is put the bag outside your door at eight every night and somebody comes by and picks it up."

"How do you know this?" she asks, walking out to the studio, half dreading the answer. It's one thing to be guarding a rickety pier from nonexistent threats, but he wouldn't have also taken on a custodian's job, would he? At his age? Things can't be that bad.

He doesn't answer her, at least not exactly. Instead he reaches for the glass she's holding towards him. "What do you do with your trash?" he asks. For some reason she's poured wine for them both. She did it automatically, without thinking, and now she's offering him a drink, even though she knows that this is cruel. She's playing a dangerous game.

"I roll the can out to the road Thursday morning like everybody else with pride and a good back," she says. "It's a pain pushing those wheels through the sand, but I figure if you're the one who makes the trash it's your job to take it out."

He considers the glass of wine she had given to him. Sniffs at it but he doesn't put his nose deep enough into the bowl and she suspects it's an affectation. Something that he saw one time, probably on television. It's not that they're trying to impress each other, not exactly. It's way too late in the day for that. But they are each trying very hard not to make the other one worry about them.

"Well you know what they say," he finally ventures. "The Point is the point."

That's definitely what they say. A billboard with that very slogan is the first thing you pass when you roll off the barrier bridge, but yet the very thought makes her bristle.

"I fought it, you know?" she tells him, watching him take the first deep gulp of her fifty-dollar cabernet and then matching him, ounce for ounce. "When those cocky bastards first got their permits and it became clear what all that digging was going to do to the bay, I picketed every day from eleven to one. Got on the local news channel more than once. Every time another bill came up for expansion I was down at the courthouse, filing an ordinance."

He chuckles softly. "And despite all that, your name's on the side of the building."

"Well yeah," she says. "I'm famous. Haven't you heard?" They both laugh, then she drinks again. He doesn't.

"Well as I see it, The Point is pretty much the opposite of the point," she says. "Last time I was up there I saw a bunch of Yankees in this shop, all of them buying candles that smelled like the beach when the real beach was right outside the door and I said to myself 'No wonder this country's going to hell in a handbasket' and then some twelve year old who called herself Wren who was working in the rooftop cafe took it upon herself to charge me fifteen dollars for a drink that was mostly cranberry juice in a skinny glass. No more than a splash of gin went into that thing, I'm telling you. I bet that child didn't give me an ounce."

"Sea Breeze."

"What?"

"That's what they call cranberry juice and gin, a Sea Breeze."

"I think I used to know that."

"And they're half price if you go at Happy Hour, from 4-6. You were just too late."

*He tends bar? He picks up trash? How has he been living all these years? How does he know these things?*

"More likely, I was too early. I generally jump the gun. I'm the kind of person who tends to show up and leave before happy hour even starts. Don't laugh. Back when we first met, I used to be one person. Now I'm another."

He drains his glass with a single swig and hands the empty back to her.

*I'm too old for this,* she thinks, out of nowhere, because she's still not totally sure that this man is actually standing in her studio or that any of what seems to be happening actually is. She's been dreaming more vividly than ever of late.

But she turns, a glass in each hand, and moves back to the kitchen. Pulls the cork from the bottle and watches the dark red liquid slowly gurgle its way into his glass then tops off her own. These two glasses are the only survivors of what was once an expensive set of eight. She scoops both up, then pauses long enough to really feel the heft in her hands, her fingers curled around each bowl. A gift from someone– most likely the woman who owns the gallery that sells all her paintings.

She steps slowly and cautiously across the floor and then holds one of the glasses out to him. She hasn't paid attention to whose was whose. She may be handing him her glass, with her germs on the rim, but he plucks it by the stem, going to great pains to avoid touching her, and raises it in a toast.

"I shouldn't be doing this," she says.

"Doing what?" he asks. "What are we doing?"

"I've got no call giving you alcohol."

"Shit, woman. Wine hardly counts as alcohol. You got gin? I can make you a Sea Breeze and it won't cost you no fifteen dollars."

She starts to tell him to sit. A better woman would tell him to sit. To make himself comfortable while she gets the gin. Because of course she's got a bottle, the decent British stuff, and there's cranberry juice in the fridge as well because women her age are prone to...never mind. This isn't the time to think about urinary tract infections or all the flotsam and jetsam of their long lives. She watches him drain the glass again, throwing back her $48 cabernet like it was nothing but $4 plunk and she feels a flicker of irritation even though she knows he's done nothing wrong. That he's been kinder to her than she's been to him and that this visitation, real or not, is a blessing she hasn't earned at all.

"I've got gin," she says. "And you may as well sit down."

"You sure? Could be risky. If we drink gin we might talk. If we talk we might tell the truth. And we both know that an hour of honest conversation could be enough to pull us right under."

She knows he's right. Forget the sharks. Forget the surf and the tides and the undertow. Memories are the most dangerous thing on the beach.

****

It might have struck Amy as strange if she'd taken two seconds to stop and think about it. Why would the development board have hired an interior decorator before the buildings had any interiors? Even the first structure on the point is no more than pipes and mortar at this point, without a drab of drywall anywhere in sight. She believes Brian might have mumbled something about having a model condo for prospective buyers to tour, and needing this model to come across top notch at the prices they were asking. But decorating a single unit with a bunch of shells and driftwood isn't enough to require a woman to drag her butt south and stay on the coast from Christmas to summer.

Sheila is her name. Amy's almost sure of it. Brian's mentioned her once or twice, in passing. Sheila from New York. A top dollar kind of decorator, he'd said. A little bit full of herself, inclined to make a fuss about her fish being broiled and her vegetables steamed and she wears entirely too much makeup to a breakfast meeting, but she's worth every penny they're paying her. So it was Sheila who'd taken Amy's green silk robe and cooked with exotic spices. Sheila who, come to think of it, must have been the source of the NYU t-shirt Brian had been wearing the day Amy and the kids finally got here.

"Where'd you get that thing?" she'd asked him and he'd looked down and shrugged, then picked up Merry and swung her around as if she was no more than a five-year-old. She's always been his favorite. Like a lot of manly men, Brian demands too much from his sons but dotes on his daughter. "Don't know why," he told her once, on a night he was deep in his cups and thus inclined to honestly. "Don't know why I find Merry the easiest one to love."

"Of course you know," she'd said. His own daddy had done the same. Pounded on his boys and Brian wouldn't live long enough to please that old man. There are times when, almost against her will, Amy remembers it all- what they were like when they first got married and how far back they go together.

There are times when she thinks all the way back to the beginning and still loves him, just a little, and then there are times like this when she could joyfully crack his head with a golf club or wrap the lines of that sailboat that he insisted on buying- even though it turns out he can't sail- around his suntanned neck.

He's the one she should be mad at. That's what she tries to remember as she walks across the rutted parking lot toward the model. Brian's the one who made her a promise, not this Yankee decorator whose door she's pounding on now. *If this were a movie,* Amy thinks, *Brian would open this tasteful, subtle, pale gray louvered door, with a towel wrapped around his waist and his hair all mussed and the scent of sex in the air and he would be once and surely caught.*

But this isn't a movie so the only person who opens the door is a blonde woman whose haircut Amy spontaneously admires, and she likes her tunic top too, damn it, and even the hanging silver discs of her earrings. It would be so much easier if she could mock this woman. If she could feel superior to her in a glance, but such isn't the case. *If she sat beside me at a school fundraiser, I'd strike up a conversation,* Amy thinks. *If we wound up in the same book club we might be friends.*

"You're Sheila?" she says. Her voice squeaks.

Sheila nods. She's taken in the measure of Amy just as Amy was looking at her and nothing seems to have raised any alarm bells. She clearly thinks Amy is the persnickety wife of a man thinking to buy one of the condos. Or maybe even take a floor of them for resale, like some investors do. She clearly thinks Amy has come to talk decorating, to look at little squares of pewter and brass. She holds out a hand to shake. Amy ignores it.

"My name's Amy," she says. "Or maybe I should say I'm Brian's wife."

To her credit, Shelia adjusts quickly. She glances toward the construction workers to make sure nobody's close enough to be listening but she doesn't invite Amy inside the model. Instead, she leans against the doorframe, looking pensive, but calm.

"Before you go any further," Sheila says, "I just want to tell you that you've won."

146

She won? How could she win a contest she didn't know she was in?

The woman makes a gesture- points towards the half-finished alley that will someday be shops and restaurants, galleries and cafes. "I built it but you can have it."

"Have it?"

"All of it. The promenade and the plaza and the tower, of course. The tower's the clincher. Consider it yours."

Amy looks at her more closely and realizes that the woman's sniffling. That her makeup –and for the record there's not too much of it, what a weird thing for Brian to say– is smudged a little just in the corner of one eye. The bright turquoise tunic Sheila is wearing is lightweight, but still too hot for a Carolina summer and obviously expensive. Not from around here. Amy knows all about expensive clothes from around here and this isn't them. Just a little more proof that this girl her husband's been boning isn't South Carolina rich, she's New York city rich, but it doesn't matter. All women look alike when they've been crying.

Amy feels a sudden and irrational impulse to hug her.

"He's not going to leave," Sheila says softly. "Once upon a time, way back in the winter, he told me he was going to. He hates this place. Do you have any idea how much he hates it? He told me that this whole town, this whole coast...It smells like failure to him."

Well, this is news. "Failure?" Amy asks skeptically. That's a word she's never even heard Brian say.

"He said just because you were born in a town, that doesn't mean it's your home," Sheila says. She wipes a single tear away carefully, with a fingertip, seemingly unaware she's already smudged her eyeliner.

Amy wipes her own cheek in an echo, even though she's not the one crying. "If he hates it so bad," she says, "then why doesn't he just pick up and leave?"

"He told me he's not the sort of man who breaks hearts. He looked me right in the eye- I think he may have still been inside of me when he said it. It was over but he was still in me. You know how they are. It takes them a while to slip out." The woman blows her nose and makes a little snorting sound. "What he meant is that he's not the sort of man who'll break your heart. Yours and the kids. He doesn't care about my heart."

This is a lot to absorb. "Are you seriously trying to tell me that my husband is breaking your heart?"

"I love him."

"I'm sorry this whole thing happened," Amy says. Sheila looks at her strangely. The wife isn't supposed to apologize to the mistress. And Amy isn't sorry in any particular way, she's just sorry for them all. She never knew Brian hated Elliott Point. Has he truly stayed here all these years just for her? She looks out into the plaza that will soon be a miniature city. The builders have gotten a bit further with that part. Tiles have already been embedded in the bronze adobe walls. Not like the hand painted tiles you get for a song in Mexico, but large squares, with subtle irregular designs. She thinks Brian told her they imported them from somewhere. She guesses he means Sheila imported them.

The woman follows her gaze. Yes," she says. "Moroccan. Rare and elegant and three times the price of the crap you pick up on the Yucatan. But you know Brian. He insists on the best."

****

Halfway back from her walk to the point, Josie piles her keys and shirt and shoes in the sand and wades into the water with just her bra and shorts on. A bra is as good as a swimsuit top, she reasons, especially this time of day when practically everyone has already moved off the beach, heading in for showers and dinner. Even the lone lifeguard in the distance is pulling his high white chair back into the dunes and waiting for the shore patrol jeep to pick him up.

Like lots of beach people, Josie's not much of a swimmer. She didn't used to go in at all but that changed abruptly twenty-three years ago. Twenty-three years ago, exactly on this day, the longest of the year, something inside of her abruptly shifted and ever since then she's felt an almost magnetic draw to the water. Not just the ocean. It was like after that particular day she couldn't stop herself from entering every body of water she encountered. Paddling, swimming, diving. Once she even waded into a fountain outside a fancy restaurant. Just stepped in, high heels and all, ignoring her friends calling out for her to stop. Muttering among themselves that she never could resist making a scene- but even now she can't say why she did it. She was knee deep in the cold gurgling water of the fountain before she turned back toward the circle of women and saw at once in their faces that this time she'd finally gone too far.

Since then she's always swam alone. And when she dives into the ocean, it's with her eyes open, not minding the sting of the salt or even the fact that the murk makes it hard to see her own hand in front of her face. If somebody asked her what she was looking for Josie would struggle to answer, but she's been looking for it quite some time.

Today she wades in slowly, steadily, walking until the gently swelling waves come almost to her chest. *Saltwater cures everything*, she says out loud to herself. Saltwater and time.

If Elliott Point had an official town cocktail, that'd be it. Pour yourself some warm saltwater into a glass and let fifty years go by and guess what, baby girl? Pretty soon you're gonna be feeling just fine.

When she was in the phone booth down at the point she'd called her son and he told her just what she expected him to tell her. That if she was all that determined to live on Elliott she should break a couple of CDs and buy a condo. Restoring a cottage at her age is too much, he'd said. As he was rambling on about helping her get the money out of Merrill Lynch and call a realtor, Josie had turned, pressed her forehead against the cool glass of the phone booth and she'd thought she'd seen Amy, just for a minute. Amy parking her car and walking fast. Amy looking angry.

"Mama, give it up. Seriously. Come home." That's what her daughter had said five minutes later, when Josie had called her.

"This is home," she'd said and then she'd looked through the glass walls of the booth again and this time, on the other side, she'd seen Clio and that rich boyfriend of hers. He'd been holding her hand, pulling her toward the edge of the point and Josie had shuddered at the very sight of them and said it again.

"I'm trying to make y'all understand that I feel more at home here than I do anywhere else."

"Maybe so. But I can't stand to think of you down there alone."

Josie had lowered her voice. It seemed essential to reassure her. As parents age, daughters do most of the grunt work. If she gets the girl on board the boy will follow.

"And I'm not as alone as you think. I've already made friends. I sat with them just today, on the beach."

"That cottage is a pile of shit, Mom."

"Don't call it shit."

"The floor slopes."

"I don't know what you're talking about."

"When we used play ping pong back in the day...I swear Mom, the floor was crooked. Somebody'd miss and the ball would roll. If you go to the corner now and pull back the curtains, I bet you'll find twenty ping ball balls up against the wall."

"I can make something of it. I've already started to paint."

"If you say so." Then she had paused. "But, Mom. You're at an age where you have to take care of yourself."

*And that's precisely what I'm doing,* Josie thinks, still carrying on the conversation with her daughter as she inches further and further away from the shore, until she's having to bounce tippy-toe to keep her head above the surface. *Because my grandma used to say that salt water heals and my grandma's always been right about everything.*

Josie had been sitting at the kitchen table. She'd said "I want the world," and she'd been what? Fourteen or maybe fifteen? That age when girls are angry and hopeful, when it still seems that anything might happen. Her grandmother had looked over and said "Oh, don't wish for that, little girl. The world's full of pain."

Which isn't the sort of thing most people would say to a scrawny, buck-toothed girl just on the edge of womanhood, but as it turned out Josie's grandma had been right about that, just the way she was right about soaking in the ocean being the secret to healing. All you have to do is go back into that same water over and over, year after year, without expectation or agenda. Walk into it and give yourself up to its power. Drift. Laze. Float.

And if that can't save you, nothing will.

Josie leans back. She lets the tide carry her, even though it's getting late and the beach is emptying and only a fool swims alone at sunset. She looks down into the murky water covering her bra, her chest, her scar, and she remembers the last thing she said to her daughter before they hung up the phone.

"I love you darling, but I've got to go. Someone's at the door."

It wasn't a lie. At least not a complete lie. Granted, she had been in a phone booth. Granted, no one was knocking and she had another mile's walk back to her cottage and granted, her main goal had only been to reassure the girl and to shut her up. But in a broader sense she hadn't lied.

There really is a door in Josie's life and there really is someone getting ready to walk through it.

She just didn't say that it was her.

****

As proposals go, this one sucks.

Jack drives her out to the point. Takes both of her hands into both of his and they stumble their way across the soft sand toward the concrete retaining wall, him going backward and her going forward. Refusing to let go of her even for an instant. He's probably just trying to be romantic but it's all so awkward and unnecessary, Clio thinks. Like they're having to work together to carry something neither one of them can see.

He stops twenty feet short of the wall and releases her.

"Daddy says you have to stand back to really get a sense of the whole thing," he tells her. He has to shout to be heard above the wind.

156

"To get a feel for the scope and...the majesty. What do you call that, when you have to keep your distance from something to really see it? When the closer you get, the less you understand?"

He doesn't wait for her to answer. He just throws his arms open wide like a game show hostess. And the view is indeed beautiful. Awe inspiring, really. The way this little jut of everyday land has somehow found the gumption to push itself right into the middle of the ocean. Water on both sides, so that anyone living out here could see the sun come up on their left in the morning and set on their right every night. Clio may not have traveled much in her short lifetime but even she knows there aren't many places like this in the world. Jack grins like a kid and she can't stop herself from grinning back.

"Perspective," she yells. "That's the word you're looking for. How you have to stand back from something to really see it."

"You can have it," he says.

"Have what?" Perspective?"

"You can have all of it. You can be the queen of all you survey."

She isn't really surprised. Everybody at the restaurant knows the two of them have been building up to this moment, even the dishwashers who barely speak English. So she isn't really surprised and yet she is, in that way you always are when the day you knew was coming finally gets here.

"I can have this view?"

"This view. The point. The high-rises that are going to be built on it." He stops yelling and drops his chin like a shy little boy, unsure of himself for the first time. "You can have me."

"Are you proposing?"

"Everybody seems to think it's time for me to get married."

Clio licks her lips. "I repeat...is this my proposal?"

Now the women of the world may not agree on everything but there are certain truths that all females, no matter their race or creed or age instinctively understand, and among these is surely the fact that if you have to flat out ask a man "Is this my proposal?" then what you're in the midst of is a shitty proposal.

*He could at least get down on one knee,* Clio thinks, even though she knows the ground beneath them is nothing but tar and pebbles and Jack is wearing white linen pants. If he'd tried to kneel she would have stopped him, but still. He should have tried. *We've got nothing in common,* she thinks. *Nothing.* Although that's a pointless point as well since Clio's lifetime ambition has pretty much been to marry a man with whom she has nothing in common. A man who can wear white pants to work and throw his arms wide and offer her a view like this. The sun coming up on one side and going down on another.

*Think, Clio, think. This is no time to get stupid.*

"Doesn't it look like a proposal? Maybe this will help."

He extends his hand and dear God, he's got a ring. Not just any old ring. A rock. He still isn't down on one knee but somehow that's mattering a little less now that Clio's seen the diamond. The sun hits the ring box and bursts Jack's badly-stated offer into a prism of possibility. Blue and purple and rose are bouncing all over the palm of his hand and

Clio stands stock still, momentarily blinded. She's moved heaven and earth to get to this moment. This. Is. The. Moment. The one all women dream about and so few of them get. What the hell's wrong with her? Why is she standing here paralyzed, like a dummy, worried about whether or not this handsome rich boy is getting down on one knee?

*Dupree would kneel,* she thinks. *Even after having me left and right and up one side and down the other, even after doing it in trucks and showers and on inflatable rafts and the pew of a Baptist church. All that said and done, when the time came for sealing the deal, Dupree would still get down on one knee to propose.* Which is nothing but country manners, the result of being raised on that strange Southern combination of moonshine and hope. Clio's smart enough to know that just the act of kneeling wouldn't be enough to make Dupree the right man.

Not to mention that he's never asked her.

"Is it the ring?" Brian asks, confused by her hesitation. He's still standing straight up, looking her eye to eye but he's holding out the box with quite a flourish, she has to give him that. Freely offering her a piece of jewelry probably worth more than her daddy's whole trailer. "Because if you don't like this particular design, you can pick out any of them you want. God knows, Mama has plenty. She just thought this one would look best on your finger. 'She has a dainty hand,' Mama said. 'So we need to find her a dainty ring.'"

"Your Mama knew you were going to propose?"

"Of course. Daddy too."

His daddy isn't the problem. His daddy started from nothing, same as Clio, and shows up almost every night at the restaurant just to check on the till, even though everybody knows he doesn't have to. His daddy once pulled Clio aside and said he could see she was a hard worker and she could tell by the tone of his voice that he considered this the highest compliment one person could pay to another. He may as well have anointed her head with oil.

No, Jack's daddy is a man who's come far but never forgot his beginnings, so the problem isn't the daddy, it's the mama, a woman born to a tiny bit more. Just a tiny bit- wasn't her papa a county manager? Or something with the farm bureau? Never mind, the point is that thirty years ago when that woman received her own proposal she must have smelled the ambition in Jack's daddy and known he was her ticket to ride and then, God love her, she rode him. All the way to a fine brick house with a circle drive and what apparently looks to be a buffet of diamond rings and yet, and yet...

And yet nobody's any snobbier than a small-town semi-socialite with just a snippet worth of status to lose and Jack's mama is the one who's filled her three sons with this same sense of entitlement. Summer sweaters and fast cars and private schools and enough confidence that they don't even have to drop to a knee to propose to a girl, at least not a girl like Clio.

"Go on, take it," he says. "I can't wait to tell her. She'll be thrilled."

Now this is highly debatable. Jack's mama undoubtedly expected something more along the line of a sorority debutante for her middle son, not some waitress come to town for the season, unbuttoning her second button just for tips and paying $22 a week to squat in a clapboard cottage in the dunes.

*Think, Clio. Stop for a minute and think.*

Because on the other hand, during her thirty years of marriage this haughty self-impressed woman has managed to birth nothing but boys and that fluke of biology has left her vulnerable. The oldest one is rumored to be a bit light in his loafers, with at least enough sense to go to Savannah for his schooling and stay there. And the youngest one they say is "special," which can mean many things, but none of them good. Clio's only hope is that Jack's mother has perused her options and is willing to take any road, even a dirt road, just so long as it leads to a big society wedding and grandchildren and she's probably smart enough to figure out that a daughter-in-law like Clio is going to show up already knowing her place. That she won't rock the boat and yet, even while she's thinking that she needs to suck up to Jack's mama, suck up to her hard, Clio can feel herself shaking her head. Like her body knows what's happening better than her mind.

"I want to get married on the beach."

Jack wrinkles his brow. "Outside?"

"Well, yeah. That's where the beach is. It's outside."

He laughs. "Barefoot? Like some kind of beatnik? While the sun is coming up?"

"We don't have to get married first thing in the morning. Maybe while the sun is going down."

He's squinting, clearly confused. "You're sure?"

"Are you sure your mother wants this?"

"My mother thinks -"

"I know, I know. Your mother thinks it's time for you to get married. That doesn't mean she has her heart set on somebody like me."

"I love you," he says.

"I love you too. And I love this view. Tell me I can wake up to this every day of my life."

A beat of silence. Then he smiles. "I'll build you the finest house on Elliott. And nothing will ever come between you and this view."

She nods, even though for some reason she's started thinking of the sand castle she'd found waiting at the bottom of her cottage steps. Dupree probably had heaped it together just to kill time while he was waiting for her to drag up from the beach. She'd hardly glanced at it as she'd passed. But she seems to recall it as a fine thing, small but carefully wrought, with a series of delicate purple shells spaced around the turret pretending windows. All the shells had been same size and color. Finding a handful of them so much alike couldn't have been easy.

Clio thinks of all that and then she looks at the other man in her life, the one standing before her now. Notes the way that even when the wind ruffles his hair it seems to drop right back into place. He shakes the ring box toward her. "So what's your answer? Are you going to be the Mistress of Elliott Point, or aren't you?"

"I don't know," Clio says.

"You don't know?"

"I'm going to have to think about it."

His brow wrinkles. This was clearly the very last thing he expected her to say.

****

The sunset side of the point may be blindingly bright, but as she walks out to her van, Amy can still see the glimmering outline of Jack holding something out to Clio. A ring, no doubt, so it looks like the girl is right on the verge of getting what she always claimed she wanted. But isn't it strange he isn't on one knee?

*He should have knelt,* Amy thinks. *It's the worst of all possible signs that on today of all days, he still won't bend his knee before her.*

She's so preoccupied with the strangeness of Clio's proposal that it takes her a moment to notice the fact Sheila's come out behind her. The woman who's just agreed, without prompting, to do the right thing. To send Brian back to his wife and three children and return to New York, where she will undoubtedly soon be decorating other women's houses and sleeping with other women's husbands. Even though Amy can hear the louvered door of the model close with a sigh, even though she knows her husband's mistress is standing right behind her with something to say, she can't seem to tear her eyes away from the young couple standing so close to the retaining wall.

As Amy watches, Clio accepts the small ring box from the man in front of her. Takes it, considers it, then clicks it shut and hands the gift back to him.

Well, that's a turn of events. The pretty rich boy evidently thinks so too. He shoves his hands into his pocket and stumbles back, as if whatever Clio just said has literally knocked him off his feet. Part of Amy wants to cheer the nerve of that little country girl, even though the rest of her, the more practical part, knows that it's only a matter of time before Clio comes around to a yes. Clio might sort of love the boy backing away from her but what she really loves is this beach.

And love makes fools of us all.

Amy whirls around, faces the still-weeping Sheila.

"You can have him," she says. "If you say he's unhappy and he feels stuck here, well then all right, I believe you. I've never been one to keep a man from his true calling."

Sheila seems stunned, almost as stunned as Jack was when Clio snapped shut the box that held his ring. For a moment hope plays across her face, as skittish as sunlight on water. Then it fades.

"That's nice," she says, "but the decision isn't ours to make. Brian's taking me to Brewster's tonight. It's my swan song. He's going to tell me goodbye and come back to you."

"Brewster's," Amy says. "Lord, girl, pull up your pride and your panties and don't let him dump you at Brewster's. That place is a fucking dive."

Sheila shrugs. "It's not so bad. I've been there before."

"So have I," Amy says. "More times than I care to count."

Brewster's is a little round-roof hovel of an establishment, tucked under the bridge connecting Elliott Point to the mainland. The sort of bar that needs those squat web-sided candles even at high noon, a place where the carpet squishes when you walk and the beer glasses vibrate whenever a truck crosses above. It's huddled among a line-up of other suspect enterprises- unlicensed fishing charters and a tattoo parlor, three bars, a motorcycle mechanic and a pop-top camper with a sign in the window saying "Therapeutic massage, pay by the minute." There have been times through the years when Amy has wondered if the whole world beneath the bridge is a sort of reverse fairyland- a portal between this plane and the one beyond with trolls and gnomes getting ready to spill through the doors at any minute.

Sheila sniffles. "That's how I know it's over. Brewster's is where you go to get rid of people you never should have been with in the first place." Which shows more Carolina smarts than a New York city girl has any right to claim and Amy has that strange thought again- that under different circumstances the two of them might have been friends. That they're not really working at cross purposes, no matter how it might seem to an outsider.

"I've got to go," Amy says. "It's suppertime. The kids need their pizza."

Because that's what being 37 is. Your whole world can collapse, the life you carefully built can crumble in the course of a single afternoon, you can find yourself the laughing stock of the yacht club, a joke among people you once thought of as sort-of your friends and in the end, none of it matters.

You still have to go home and feed the kids.

****

"Now that one's real fine," he says, pointing toward one of her paintings with the toe of his scruffy tennis shoe. "Looks just like when the sun comes out after a storm."

"Do you want it? You can take it if you want it."

He snorts. "You expect me to just go walking down the beach with a picture of the beach stuck under my arm?"

170

"Well, not stuck under your arm," she says, wondering why on earth she would offer something she couldn't deliver. She can't send him off with a painting, or at least not that one. She was working on it earlier today. It's still wet.

"But it's got a mistake," he says, pointing with his foot again. "You put a shadow where there ain't nobody there."

She starts to explain herself, to go into the kind of bullshit speech she gives to libraries and garden clubs, to say that maybe the shadow belongs to someone standing beyond the perimeters of the painting. To say that maybe this smear of shade is thrown by the painter herself, the unseen person in every picture. Or she could go full-out artsy on him and spout some sort of gobbledygook about shadows representing our unlived lives. Because we all have them- whole other existences we might have stumbled upon if we'd only turned left instead of right, if we'd driven on instead of stopping, if we'd swallowed a birth control pill instead of that last shot of vodka, if we'd blurted out what we were thinking instead of smiling and nodding just one more time. As we age, as we slow down, it gets harder and harder to outrun these unlived lives. They nip at our heels, she could have told him. They follow us close as a dog on a leash.

But this man has lived with enough pain already. She can see it in his face, so Cully figures the Christian thing is to give him a less complicated answer.

"You're right, it's a mistake," she says. "Just a smudge of paint I tried to cover up with another color, but I think I just made it worse. You know what they say on the news shows," she adds with a little hiccup. "The cover-up's generally worse than the crime."

He nods slowly and -there's no other word for it-soberly before he drains the second glass. "Never really considered you the kind to make a mistake."

"Please."

"All right then. Never really considered you the kind to admit to a mistake."

Cully turns abruptly. "Want me to top you off? I can open another bottle."

"Oh, I dare not. Don't look at me like that, for I truly dare not. You've already led me this far down the road to perdition, but I've got a long walk ahead, not to mention a dog still tied to your railing."

The thought of him walking home alone pains her. The yacht club basin must be three miles away and you have to cross that high bridge, him with a belly full of high-priced cabernet, thanks to her, and most likely little else. The circumstances under which he must be living have started to come to back to her more and more the longer he's stood here talking. She'd seen that hut at the end of the pier years ago and it was a ramshackle affair even then, designed to be used for an hour at a time, if that. Certainly never meant for permanent habitation. Most likely it was given to him by the members of the yacht club more out of pity than anything else and he's got to know that. The charity probably stings more than salt spray on a scraped leg and yet he stays out there, all alone, year round, including the winter. Does the place even have a full bath or a kitchen?

"I could drive you home," she blurts out.

"You got a car?"

"No, but I still have my license. I can borrow one from a neighbor or somebody and drive you home."

"We both know that ain't wise."

Cully looks at the clock on the wall and nods. Enough "ain't wise" things have already happened and when she looks back he's moving toward the door. There's no suggestion of a hug.

She watches him go down the steps. Slow and steady as a clock. He unhooks his dog from where he left it, with the leash loosely draped around the banister of her deck. The creature could have escaped anytime he'd wanted, Cully thinks, but the dog is as old and tired as his master. He stands up with an air of resignation, shakes off the sand and prepares for the long shuffle home. Cully lingers in the doorframe, unable to turn away just yet, and sure enough the two figures pause when they get to the top of the first dune. The man takes a moment to collect his breath and she waits for him to look back at her.

But he doesn't. He just stands there a moment and then he keeps walking. It's not until he's almost at the top of the second dune that she calls out.

"You know," she says. "I've painted 846 paintings in my life. I keep count. I write it down in a book. And when I started out in the beginning most of them were pure shit but since then, since I've gotten better and become..."

Now he turns. She thinks he's even smiling. "You've become a real artist."

"Well I don't know about that. But as of last week I've somehow managed to sell 619 of those 846 paintings despite the fact every damn one of them has the same mistake."

"The shadow of somebody who ain't really there."

"Exactly," she says, stepping back inside, letting the screen door go with a slam. "But you're the first person who's ever noticed."


****

Something brushes against her and Josie cries out. She looks around, but sees nothing. Since she started swimming like this -late in the afternoon and alone- Josie's been stung by jellyfish more times than she can count. Once she got caught in a riptide that pulled her parallel to the shore for better than twenty minutes before it released her from its grip, almost as if the angel of death had gotten bored with her and gone off to hunt more interesting prey. A skate grazed against her on another occasion, and she's even been head-butted by a dolphin, although nobody believes that story when she tells it.

But all any swimmer really fears are the sharks. They may be statistically unlikely, far rarer than lightning strikes and true love and lottery wins, but still. They're sharks. We can know damn well that certain things are statistically unlikely and somehow they still haunt our dreams.

The sky has become streaks of rose and gold, and Josie's thoughts jerk back, as they have all day, to that pair of boys that stole from her. They know she's staying in that little cottage all alone and that she has some items of value randomly scattered among the wreckage of her life. They know she winces when she lifts her arms over her head and there's nothing to stop them from coming back.

Josie looks at the sky and tries to talk some sense into herself even though she's been lost in this kind of random free-floating vulnerability pretty much nonstop since the diagnosis. All those treatments and even the word "remission" haven't done much to make her feel safe. Cancer's like those young foster boys- a thief has her address. It could pull into her driveway at any point and steal something else from her, because once trouble knows where to find you, it never forgets.

All of the sudden the water feels colder, the way beach water sometimes does. She's floated into a tide within a tide and Josie shudders, flails for a moment, before she realizes she's drifted out further than she'd thought. Her toes no longer graze the ground when she tries to stand and a surge of adrenalin hits her. She twists right and left but doesn't see the dreaded fin, the one we all expect, and she resolutely starts breast-stroking in the direction of the shore.

But she hardly gets in four good scoops of water before she feels it again. That same rough sensation, now brushing against her thigh. First one leg and then the other. It's not a fish. Nothing alive at all, just something floating. She pulls up, relieved to feel that the balls of her feet are touching sand, at least between the swells of waves, then reaches down and grabs with both hands.

It takes a slow and steady effort to pull the thing up but when she does she can see that she's become tangled in a scrap of canvas. It's heavy but when she tugs at it, the white shape undulates behind her, almost as if she's being followed by a ghost. Half-swimming and half-walking, she manages to keep it in her arms as she continues to move toward land. Soon enough she finds a sandbar. Stands on it for a minute to give her heartbeat time to slow and let her take a closer look at the fabric in her hands.

What she's holding is just a scrap of torn sail, nothing more.

Nobody has any use for a torn sail. She doesn't even own a boat. But for some reason she decides to bring it all the way to shore.

****

"You told him no?"

"What I told him is that I'm not sure."

"Not sure?" says Jeannie. She's practically yelling, leaning in so far that Clio can feel her breath. "He's rich and he's cute and he's crazy about you. How the hell can you not be sure?"

Clio wipes back a stray hair with her forearm. "I don't know. I can't think. Just let me finish out the rest of my shift."

Jeannie dumps a tray's worth of empty Budweiser bottles into the trash. "Finish out your shift? If you marry the boss's son you'll never have to work another shift the rest of your life, you do get that, don't you? Pop out a kid or two and you'll be sitting pretty."

"It isn't exactly like that."

"Then what's it like?" Jeannie cuts her eyes toward Clio. "People raised hard, like me and you...Don't lie. We both know who we are. We both know damn well that some girls can drive themselves straight into one ditch after another and every time they do it a hundred angels will reach down off their clouds and pull them back on the road and, bibbedy bobbedy boobedy, it'll be like nothing even happened. The dirt and the pain and the shame will roll right off of them because that's the way they were born. Some girls get college and trips to Europe and abortions and...and, you know, redemption and stuff. But people like me and you- how many chances to do you figure people like me and you get?"

"One."

"If that."

Clio shakes her head. Tries to shake it all off because, like it or not, Jeanne's only speaking hard truth. "I didn't exactly tell him no. What I told him-"

"Jesus, Mary, Joseph, what's he doing back?"

Jeanne jerks her head toward the big picture glass window overlooking the bay and Clio follows her gaze to the sight of Dupree's truck, bouncing down the sandy road toward the restaurant. Just looking at that beat up Ford, going too fast like it always does, is enough to make her queasy, but she forces herself to shrug.

"Finished his run and came back for one of your pity beers, I guess."

"How much does he know?"

"There's nothing to know." Clio puts the last Big Catch Platter on her tray.

"I'm asking you if Dupree is aware that he's getting ready to lose his summer girl," Jeannie whispers, slapping her own plates down on the tray so hard that the hushpuppies bounce every which way.

"He doesn't know about the ring, if that's what you're asking" Clio says. "Nobody does. Nobody but you, that is."

Jeannie makes a face like she's about to say something else and then thinks the better of it. She bends her knees in that steady waitress swivel and picks up her order, which is even heavier and stacked higher than Clio's. And then Jeannie stands up then snaps the tray stand shut with her free hand.

"I still can't believe you told him no," she mutters as heads toward the main dining room.

"What I told him is that I'd think about it," Clio says softly, turning away from the window before she has to watch Dupree getting out of that truck.

\*\*\*\*

"I've been thinking," Josie says.

"A highly dangerous activity," says Cully. "I never recommend it." She's back out on the beach now and a bit surprised to find Josie here, soaking wet, and sitting beside her. The woman all but washed ashore a few minutes ago, wearing a wet bra and dragging a piece of beat up fabric behind her, babbling something about a message from

God, which in itself is news. Cully wouldn't have figured Josie to be the religious sort.

"So what sort of thinking are we talking about?" she asks, more gently this time. The lights on the point are starting to come on now, one at a time. A hundred little rectangles of gold and silver, glittering in the blue-black sky.

"It's occurred to me that whatever age you happen to be at the moment, you're all the other ages you've ever been too. A woman can be sixteen and sixty at the same time."

"Hell, girl, I could've told you that. You had to half drown to come to that conclusion?"

"I didn't half drown."

"You don't look too hot."

"But it's all sort of depressing, isn't it?" Josie asks, rocking from one hip to the other, feeling the sand shift and sink beneath her. "To think that nobody really ever escapes whatever they're trying to get away from? That nobody ever really gets over anything?"

"We cannot change," Cully says grandly. "But we can expand."

"Who said that?"

"I'm not sure. I think it was Napoleon."

"Are you sure? It doesn't sound like Napoleon." When Cully doesn't say anything Josie shifts her weight again. The sand bar is loosening with the pull of the receding water. She's not sure how Cully's even keeping her chair in place but the woman is perched there like some sort of aquatic goddess, immovable by the vagaries of mere tides. "Why'd you come back out? Isn't it time for your Jeopardy? Please don't tell me you're planning to stay out here past dark."

Cully looks up. "Are you?"

"No. Not at all. In fact, I think I'm going to go back to my house and paint something. Now please don't laugh. It won't be much. Nothing professional, nothing like you do. I just want to sort of play around, maybe have a little-"

"Experiment."

"Exactly. An experiment. And it's likely to fail because most experiments do. But I was thinking if it didn't fail completely that maybe I'd do more of them, you know? That I could paint seascapes on canvas from reclaimed sails and people might like that. If it comes out terrible, like, you know, all runny and blurry I could tell them it's the canvas that makes it look like that and not the artist. And the whole concept would be sort of different, you know?"

"Different."

"Oh I know it sounds silly to somebody like you. Somebody established and serious and famous. But I have to do something to keep myself busy or I'll go insane. And it would be nice to make a little bit of money. Nothing like you can ask for a painting, of course. I'm not even trying to be notable...or deep. I just need a little hobby. And I was thinking I'd name the series-"

"Good Lord, now there's a series?"

"Well, of course not. As of this particular moment, there's not even one. But it's not like I don't have some experience with composition and visuals...and I was thinking if I picked up the knack with the paints...I know. I'm being silly. Very silly indeed and thank you for not laughing in my face, but I was thinking if I did one and it wasn't too godawful and then I did another, I could call them the Women in the Dunes series. The beach at different times of day from different angles. I mean each time the light and water shift it turns into a whole different world."

"I never noticed."

"Oh God. Sorry. Really. Look who I'm talking to. But you're an artist, Cully, a real one, and I'm just a nobody who's gotten it into her head to move down to the beach on the eve of the longest day of the year but I know damn well that sooner or later fall will be coming. Fall then winter, and I'll lose my mind, seriously, if I don't figure out something to pass the time." Josie spreads her arms as wide as they will go. "You have this much. And I'll have, maybe" -and here she holds her thumb and forefinger an inch apart- "this much. We're just talking about a hobby. A joke, really. Like you said. Let's just call it an experiment."

Cully nods. "Yep. This is exactly how it begins."


****


186

Amy walks in the kitchen to find two messages on her answering machine. She puts the pizza down, for once not caring if the circle of grease burns its way through to the counter, and then hits the blinking red button.

"Good news, babe," her husband says. She hates it when he calls her babe. It's a new thing. Probably, now that she stops to think of it, born of his affair. Brian's cagey enough to know he has to use the same endearment for the wife and the mistress. Otherwise the wrong name might slip out at a pivotal moment.

"Good news," her husband is saying. "The environmental report came back and we're golden. We finish the pilings tomorrow. Twenty-four stories, babe. Twenty-four beautiful solid gold stories so let's go shopping for that Jag this Satur-"

A beep. He's gloated so long he's cut himself off. Amy stands and waits. Another beep and he's back. "But I was calling to say I'll be late. Midnight, maybe more, so lock up and go to bed and don't worry. The guys and I are headed out to celebrate at the Grand B Social Club -"

He's gone again. The Grand B Social Club is what he calls Brewster's under the bridge, so it looks like Sheila really did tell the truth about where she was going to meet him tonight, although Amy doubts that Brian asked her there to dump her. Or if he did, it was before he knew that the bribes to the Chamber of Commerce worked. Before he was sure that good old-fashioned cash would always win out over sea turtles and nesting terns and the chants of a raggedy little crew of environmentalists carrying signs on sticks and walking back and forth in front of the county commissioner's office.

The Point is the Point. That's what he's spent the fifteen years of their marriage telling her and once the sea-rovers come in and start pushing around the sand and building retaining walls, they're going to be rich. Not Elliott Point rich but Anywhere on Earth rich and the timing is certainly strange, isn't it? Timing generally is. That here, on the very day Amy has discovered her husband has a mistress and the very day that mistress claims he is about to leave her, the ruling comes down that they can begin to build.

*He has no need to choose between me and Sheila now,* Amy thinks, looking at the phone on the counter with its brightly blinking TWO. *Now he can afford us both. Afford us just not financially but in every sense of the word.* Because while driving back from the pizza place, Amy admitted something else to herself too. It wasn't only Brian's partners and golfing buddies who knew about Sheila. Everybody in town did. Up until today the court of public opinion might have been leaning toward him having to give one of them up and Brian, always cautious, must have decided to take the path of least resistance and stay with his wife and kids.

But that was before the ruling. Before her husband, with the swipe of some bought-off bureaucrat's pen, became the richest man in the county and most likely its biggest employer as well. And key taxpayer, and most benevolent patron of worthy causes. Amy doesn't even have to shut her eyes to see it all unfolding around her. Libraries and schools and public parks with his name on them. Maybe even an oceanography museum. Some society devoted to saving local wildlife.

Because the most ironic thing about Brian is that he has absolutely no sense of irony at all.

But he knows how to throw money at trouble. He learned that early and well, which is why he's willing to buy his wife a Jag and at the same time be popping champagne with his mistress under a bridge. Does Brewster's even have champagne?

Never mind. Brian knows that if he puts this little beach on the map, brings in enough tourists to share the wealth with his neighbors, he will have bought himself so much good will that he can do whatever he likes in his personal life. Be South Carolina's personal homegrown answer to Hugh Hefner and the perfect family man all in one swoop and who around here is going to tell him that he can't?

Amy glances up the stairs. The kids are being awfully quiet. Quiet kids are one of those things that seem like good news but hardly ever are.

190

****

Josie thins the wall paint with the leftover contents of a can of turpentine and, when she finally gets the gunk somewhat liquid, she grabs an old t-shirt and balls it up. Dips it in the paint and drags it across the canvas. She's not expecting much. The sail's still wet and a t-shirt isn't meant to be a brush. Besides, while she's been messing with the paint it's gotten too dark to really see what the colors are doing.

But even in the thin light from the front porch, she can tell that her grand experiment isn't working. Everything seems just like one more shade of gray, most likely because she's being too cautious. Josie tilts the heaviest can and pours it across the sail until the paint puddles, then she does the same thing with another, all the time yanking on the corner of her makeshift canvas, watching the circles of color run together. A door slams above her and she looks up, feeling exposed. Standing out in the dunes in her jeans and her bra is absurd, especially considering she hardly ever wears her prosthesis and so she's flat on one side and hilly on the other. But it's nobody but Amy, back from whatever errand took her earlier and once again standing on her deck. She's leaning over the very edge of the railing, stretched out like Leo and Kate in that silly movie, and entirely too preoccupied to notice Josie below her on the sand.

*She's always so sad,* Josie thinks, but even in the shadows she can tell that the color is taking. Maybe even doing something interesting. She's not sure how she feels about these babyish shades of paint, or even the idea of pastels in general. Maybe she's ready for brighter colors in her life. And as for this literally washed-up sail...

*In the final analysis sails are nothing more than canvas,* Josie reminds herself. *And artists paint on canvas so there's no reason to think it won't eventually work. It's mostly about the story I'll tell future clients. And if that story happens to be hokey, all the better. Hokey sells.*

Above her, Amy screams. She's leaning against her railing screaming in the general direction of the point. Just pure screaming and Josie wonders if she should find another shirt, put it on, and walk up the stairs to try and reason with the girl. She's been off her game all day- throwing jars of spices and driving too fast and now standing up there howling like a banshee. It doesn't matter how far apart the houses around here are. If she doesn't get a grip on whatever's grieving her, she's going to ruin her reputation. She's going to scare her kids. She's going to let pain and anger take over her reason and cause her to do a foolish thing. Something way more foolish than just pouring waves of house paint over a scrap of somebody's torn sail.

****

Cully's wading in the water. Not anywhere near where they left her. She must have gone in and come back out.

Amy is a little ashamed of herself for screaming. God knows, she has problems of her own, but the sight of Cully, a little wobbly on her feet and so pitifully alone, puts the whole thing in perspective. Amy wonders if she should call down to her, maybe invite her in for a slice of pizza. It's hardly a good night for entertaining, not even in the pizza on a napkin sense, but something's not right about the fact the woman is wading knee deep, letting the tide surround her. Cully's so eccentric she could have gone purely senile without any of them recognizing it and besides, Amy would like someone to talk to tonight. Someone older, with the wisdom of the years.

But just as Amy is about to cup her hands and yell down to the beach she glances up and sees Merry watching from the French doors. Merry and Cully have always been an uneasy pair, sort of like a set of matching bookends with a whole lot of stories jammed between them. It's not that they argue, exactly, but neither one of them is afraid to speak her mind. Amy has noticed this about women- that they'll talk plain truth in the beginning, when they're girls, and then they go mute for maybe fifty or sixty years. Going along, getting along, keeping the peace until the day when, without warning, at the age of eighty or so they turn back into teenagers.

194

Ready to fight anybody over anything, crazy in love with the sound of their own voices.

"What were you hollering about?" Merry asks.

"I was singing."

"That's not singing."

"It's how I sing," Amy says, thinking that if Merry's astir, she better leave Cully where she is. Merry doesn't seem to have noticed Cully walking on the beach or even Josie below them, limping around in her bra making a hell of a lot of racket dragging things around her yard. "Dinner's on the counter."

"You mean another pizza's on the counter."

"I'm going out tonight."

"With who?"

"What do you mean, with who? With your daddy, that's who. We're going to celebrate. He's just won the legal right to poison the beach." Amy stands aside. "Better come look at this view while you still can. Next year by this time there's going to be nothing in front of us but a giant high rise."

Merry walks out slowly. "You're saying he got his permit to drive in pilings?"

"That's exactly what I'm saying."

"So we're going to be rich," the girl says slowly. Her voice reveals nothing, but she can't resist looking in the direction where her mother is pointing. "We're getting ready to turn into a whole different family than the one we are now."

Amy nods. "I guess that's one way to look at it."

\*\*\*\*

By eight-thirty, the place is packed. All the big tables in the back are full, which means double-stacked trays and beer by the pitcher. Exhausting work, but Clio isn't looking forward to her second break. In fact, she dreads it.

Clio would have kept working right through entirely if Jeannie hadn't been so persistent, coming up behind her more than once, saying that there was a lull, even when there wasn't, and telling Clio she could cover her tables if she wanted to take a minute. Each time Clio would nod, but then find something to busy herself, even cleaning off a four-top at one point, leaving the busboy standing confused right behind her until finally Jeannie said "Go on, girl. You know he's waiting to talk to you."

She means Jack, who's been working the front of house since they got back from the point. Jawing with the regulars and the money must be flowing extra good tonight because he's already taken out the canvas zip bag from under the counter and made a run to the deposit drawer at the bank. Dupree's still here too, but he's been as still as Jack is busy, taking possession of a single barstool in the corner and there he sits, drinking slow and steady, rolling an unlit cigarette back and forth between his fingers.

"You know what he said to me a minute ago?" Jeannie says, looking dreamily towards Jack, who's thrown his head back and is laughing like crazy at something an old man in the corner is saying. "He said 'Where is everybody?' and there must be a hundred people in this room. A hundred people, packed in asses to elbows, but when he says 'everybody' he's only talking about you."

Clio nods slowly.

"That's sweet, you know?" says Jeannie. "You're his everybody. So get off your high horse and go take your damn break."

Clio doesn't want to take her damn break but Jeannie's looking at her, expectant like, and she does have to pee. And so Clio heads toward the kitchen, walking straight through the cooks and the dishwashers to the back where there's a nasty little toilet tucked away. Only the guys frequent this hell hole. In fact, she bets the toilet seat hasn't been in the down position since Pearl Harbor, but she drops it and squats, holding up her skirt and staring down at the greasy floor. The waitresses usually use the ladies' room out front, even though the manager doesn't particularly like it and tells them to remember that as long as they have those puffy-sleeved shirts on, they're still representing the Spanish Moss. Be polite, he says, and let guests cut in line and don't make any noises in the stalls. If you gotta do something that might make a noise, go do that something somewhere else. Most of all, make sure all the customers see you washing your hands real good when you're done.

But Clio can't face the ladies' room out front tonight. Not with Jack working the room like a politician and Dupree drinking like it's his day job and Jeannie's eyes flicking back and forth among the three of them. Better to contort herself into the back toilet, crouching on one bent leg and using the other foot to brace the door shut, trying to hurry and then running cold water over her hands from the soapless sink. She walks back through the kitchen, ignoring that little sucking sound the dishwashers make whenever they even see any kind of a girl, and out the screen door into the parking lot. She has no plan in mind for her fifteen minutes of freedom, but they're still parked beside each other, the pick-up truck and the sports car.

For no reason she can name, she opens the door of the produce truck and climbs in. She's never sat on this front seat. Laid down in the flatbed a couple of times but that doesn't count. The cab smells like Dupree, all sweat and dirt. There's a map folded on the dashboard, which seems strange. Surely he can drive his delivery route in his sleep by now. The paper's worn so thin that it's beginning to tear in the creases. Towns getting lost in the cracks, roads sliding off into nowhere. Clio pokes a finger through one of the slits and obliterates Murrells Inlet entirely then unfolds the top section until she finds the town where she was born and raised. No more than a thumb's distance from where she sits now.

*I haven't gotten far,* she thinks. *It feels like I've crossed the world but when you look at a big map like this, three summers worth of progress don't add up to much.*

A horn honks. She jumps. Looks over her shoulder but it's only that tableful of golfers finally leaving. Well and truly drunk by now, beeping and hollering like a bunch of hoodlums before they pull out and go their separate ways. The map has dropped from her lap. Her eyes still on the golfers, Clio reaches down with one hand, patting the grimy floor underneath her seat. Her fingertips catch the soft paper and then something else, even softer, and she pulls it out.

What she's found is a bra. Red. That kind of shiny red satin that under the parking lot light pole looks closer to a cherry pink.

Now like most white trash country girls, Clio has yearned for many things in her life. Her first summer down, back when a twenty was enough to make her practically faint, she'd taken her Memorial Day tips and gone shopping. Looking back on it now, she'll freely admit that not all of those original purchases turned out to have been in the best of taste. But never, not even in the tackiest days of her early money, had she ever dreamed of purchasing a red bra. It is such a bizarre and unlikely thing to find under the passenger seat of Dupree's pick-up that for a moment Clio's mind freezes.

Then she remembers. It hadn't been that long ago, just a few weeks back at the soft opening of the summer. Her and Jeannie, in the ladies' room meant for patrons, not staff. Trying to hurry like they always were. They'd gone into a stall together and Jeannie had squatted and pulled down a pair of red satin panties. Clio had made some sort of comment. Something silly, something like "Whoo-whoo Sister," and they'd laughed, even though Clio had remembered what Jack's mother had said on one of the rare occasions she'd come into the restaurant. Some bitchy remark about how you might be able to take the girl out of the trailer park but you'd never be able to take the trailer park out of the girl.

Clio had winced at the time, sure the woman had been getting in a dig at her, but maybe she'd been talking about Jeannie all along. Jeannie who could add a whole series of tickets in her head without fail, even for the ten tops, but who was a slow learner when it came to the things that really mattered.

And it seems that the kind of girl who takes her start-of-the-season tip money to buy red panties might decide to get herself a red bra to match.

Clio opens the door to the truck. It's suddenly all hit her. The heat, the constant smell of grease and fish, the nerves she's been pushing down all day, with no success. She leans over the sandy gravel and begins to puke. First she loses the beer she'd snuck when she got back from the point, then the

202

baked potato, then the remains of a tomato sandwich she'd eaten with one hand while driving to work, until finally there's nothing left but foamy green bile. She waits for a minute to make sure it's all passed, praying no one has seen her. If Jack's daddy knew a waitress was throwing up in the parking lot of his restaurant on a crowded Friday night, Clio could stand to lose a lot more than her lunch. She sits up and uses the back of her hand to wipe first tears from her eyes and then spittle from the corner of her mouth. The map and the bra are still in her lap. She places them both on the dashboard, side by side.

*Thank you, Dupree,* she thinks, fumbling her way down from the truck seat and slowly starting back toward her work. Her work, her future... hell, her destiny, because no girl in her right mind would turn down the sort of offer Clio has been given today. No girl in her right mind would think anything but "Yes, please. Make me the boss man's son's wife and guarantee that I'll never have to hoist a tray of fourteen platters or pee in the back toilet again." As she walks through the front door, Clio's trying very hard not to think about the red bra. She's trying to focus on the fact she needs to find Jack. She'll tell him that her earlier refusal was nothing but a little game. Her playing hard to get -now there's a joke- so that he'd want her more. She's gotta find Jack and explain that they can set the date and the sooner the better. The ceremony can be held on the beach or at a church or country club, no matter to her. Whatever his mama wants. His mama can choose the bridesmaids' dresses. Hell, his mama can choose the bridesmaids. The woman may be a bitch and a snob, but Jeannie's probably right. All Clio has to do is spit out a couple of babies and she'll be golden. Once she single-handedly secures the next generation, Jack's people will have no choice but to take her into the fold.

Jack is standing near the big front windows, the ones that overlook the marsh. He glances up as she enters the main dining room, almost like he sensed her presence before he saw her. He gives her a little smile. It's tentative. Hopeful. She's his everybody, after all. She grins back and waves him over.

*Thank you, Dupree,* Clio thinks again. *And thank you, Jeannie. Thank y'all both very kindly for making this next part a whole lot easier than I thought it was going to be.*

\*\*\*\*

The thing about Brewster's is that only locals come here. Summer people couldn't begin to find the little dirt road that turns and turns and turns again, switching back and forth down the bank beneath the bridge and finally coming to rest in what, for the sake of simplicity, we may as well call a parking lot.

What Amy's getting ready to do isn't smart. An unimportant woman fixing to leave an important man needs to be strategic but what Amy's planning is more of a Statement. A broad gesture, maybe even a bit of a temper tantrum, and she'll undoubtedly pay for it in the end. Or maybe she'll be paying for it in a couple of hours. If a woman decides to take off without argument or warning in the middle of a hot Carolina night, she should at least have enough sense to be driving a minivan as she goes. You can't get much in a BMV convertible. Not much more than your kids and your pride.

A duplicate of her car key is on his ring and a duplicate of his is on hers. Not because she and Brian are so close that they share everything but more as a concession to the fact that when you have three kids who are always going in three different directions, one parent will likely be dropping them off at practice and another will be picking them up. The minivan she's driving now is roomy and convenient, but she's never liked the vehicle, not since the day Brian came home with it saying he'd picked it up on the cheap from a friend of a friend's cousin. The Mamamobile, that's what the twins call it, even when Brian's the one behind the wheel. The back is a jumble of sneakers and gymbags, a thousand empty water bottles, half-used tubes of suntan lotion, jumper cables and a couple of rusted out folding chairs for watching ball games.

Brian can have all that. She's taking the Beamer.

Which makes no sense but what part of today has? Brewster's is glowing before her. One window red, another amber, a green Budweiser lamp in the third window with the "wei" part either burned out or broken so that it only says "Bu ser." Cars are double-parked all around, with a few wedged in behind the dumpster. She'd seen Brian's convertible at once, but made no effort to pull near it. Instead she'd abandoned the van a bit further back in the parking lot, tucked close to one of the bridge pilings and Amy is now walking unsteadily in the dark toward the neon lights, willing the front door of Brewster's not to open with people walking out. It's a safe bet she knows everybody in that bar but there's not a damn one of them that she wants to see tonight.

"What on earth are you doing here?"

Someone's come up behind her. She turns and looks up at a man through blurry eyes and realizes she must be crying. She's known him half her life but for a minute she blanks out on his name. He's on the zoning board that Brian just bribed, but still- she's always thought of him as one of the good ones. A local, which means he should care about the land, and yet he must have come here to celebrate with the others. Come to Brewster's to toast the fact that any day now they're all going to be able to sell their lots and boat slips and melon farms and concrete block convenience stories for more than their daddies would have ever dreamed possible.

Amy's past the point of even trying to think of a plausible lie.

"My sorry excuse for a husband," she says, watching the man's face change just a bit as she enunciates every word, "is in that bar celebrating with his Yankee mistress. Earlier this day- it's the longest of the year, did you know that?"

"I think I heard something like that on the radio."

"The longest damn day of the year," Amy repeats. She feels drunk, even though she hasn't had a drop of alcohol and she sways a little on her feet. The man reaches out and grabs her arm. Roughly, like he thinks she's going to fall down in this nasty old parking lot, like he doesn't know that Amy has no intention of falling at all.

"Earlier this day my husband's little piece on the side called me out of a clear blue sky and so I went to the building site to meet her," she says. "She tried to tell me that Brian was going to dump her right here tonight, which was probably true at the time she said it.

Only you and your spineless committee, y'all bunch of faithless stewards...you sold the point out and now my husband is going to be rich enough to afford both a wife and a mistress. Or at least that's what he thinks."

"I take it you think he's thinking wrong?"

"Damn right. I've come here to steal his car and leave his ass."

The man pauses to consider this. "Can a woman steal her own husband's car? You have a key, don't you? Of course you do. It's right there in your hand. I guess that makes it half your car too."

"Yeah, well, I'm taking the whole thing."

He glances towards Brewster's. The others - his friends on the zoning board and Brian's friends on the development council- are undoubtedly already inside, sitting twelve men to a table, with one woman among them in the center like Jesus at the last supper. A woman wearing a turquoise tunic top with little dangling disc earrings. A woman who may be already starting to see that a twist of fate has saved her. Oh no, she's not going to be dumped tonight. She's going to keep on working to decorate those condos at the point. They'll put up another building then another one and she's going to have weeks and months and even years to worm her way into Amy's position. Because she might not know that Amy has plans to steal the Beamer and take off this very hour but Sheila surely does know that, come fall, Amy's going to have to pack up the kids for real and take them back to school in Charlotte. Leaving Sheila heir apparent to her throne.

Because that's the thing about the longest day of the year. After that there's nothing for the world to do but get a little bit darker, day after day.

"I think you'd better let me drive you home," the man says. His fingers are still gripping her forearm. "You got no call piloting any sort of vehicle in your condition."

"I'm not drunk, I swear I'm not."

"No, but you're upset. And you've got a right to be." He raises her arm with his fist and together they gesture awkwardly towards the bar. "I didn't know they were going to be here tonight. I thought they'd be anywhere but here, truth be told. Seems like they'd go somewhere fancy."

She shakes her head. "I don't need a pity lie."

"It's not pity and it's not a lie. Just let me drive you home. For everybody's sake."

"You're saying I should just leave my car here? The van and the beamer? Both of them? So you can drive me home and dump me out and then come back here to drink with all these people practically standing in line to sell out my beach? I'm sure you do. I bet you see the situation just like Brian, imagining that everybody on Elliott is going to be happy, happy, happy as shit to sell to developers and the sea turtles and the dolphins and sharks are all going to just have to go somewhere else. And the terns. Somewhere where the people aren't as smart and don't know they're sitting on a gold mine."

He opens the door of his car. It's a BMW too, she realizes. Another convertible, just a different color from her husband's. There's a joke lost in this situation somewhere, but she can't quite think of what it might be.

"Sea turtles and terns?" he says, with a chuckle. "Sounds like you're way more pissed about the beach than you are about the mistress."

"It's easier to get a new husband than it is to get a new beach," Amy says, kind of spitting the words, but she allows herself to be ushered into the passenger seat of his car. He slams the door and walks around to the driver's side, glancing at the BU SER sign in the window as he does so. She supposes she should thank him for saving her from herself but she's still full of nervous energy and annoyed that she isn't going to get to make her Statement. Brian needs to know he doesn't own quite everything on Elliott Point. Even though it might look like it, he doesn't own her.

"Just so you know, I voted against the resolution," the man says, sliding in and cranking the engine.

"Save your breath. There's no point trying to suck up to me."

He shrugs. "Look at the paper tomorrow if you don't believe me. It'll show the resolution passed eleven to one. I'm the one."

She remains silent as they bounce up the hill to the main road, the ruts throwing her first one way and then the other. When they get back to the pavement, he turns on his blinker to the left. Amy thinks for half a second and then reaches over and turns it to the right.

"Take me off the island and down to Shallotte," she says. "When I said I wasn't drunk, I should've said I wasn't drunk yet. Not near as drunk as I intend to be."

He considers the situation for a minute. Looks at her then looks at the road, first left and then right. "All right," he finally says. "I suppose a single drink is innocent enough. You just need to blow off some steam. Perfectly understandable under the circumstances. Losing your sea turtles and your husband in one day, I mean."

She nods. "And you'll drive me home afterwards, won't you? Make sure that none of what's happening here has any...you know, any consequences?"

"Absolutely," he says. "If there's one thing I hate, it's consequences."

****

"I'll marry you."

"Say it louder."

She puts her hands around her mouth like a megaphone. "I said I'll marry you."

"Alrighty then," he says. Took you long enough, but alrighty." He snaps his fingers toward the staff like he thinks he's a sheik in an old movie. "Bring on the champagne."

Clio would have bet every dime she'd saved that there never had been a bottle of champagne within the dark paneled walls of the Spanish Moss and yet here one comes, right towards her, with the whole kitchen crew marching along behind it. Even the three dishwashers wiping their hands on their aprons and wearing the sweet faces of altar boys, acting like they weren't hissing and clicking their tongues at her ten minutes ago. Jeannie's crying, for reasons Clio will have to think about later. The other serving girls are clapping their hands in that way they do to start the birthday song and the manager is laughing his fake jolly laugh and they've all circled around her, fast enough that Clio understands the champagne was already in the back, already on ice, way before Jack took her out to the point. Today when she got to work she was the only one in the building that didn't know he was going to propose. And he was sure enough of her answer to have this all ready.

"Say it again," Jack tells her. "In front of everybody."

She throws back her head, soaking in the laughter and the applause. This many people can't be wrong. Even Valerie is smiling and clapping and Valerie doesn't approve of anything.

"Yes," she says. "Yes, yes, yes. Of course I'll marry you."

A cork pops. Someone hands her the first glass, more foam than substance, and others are poured around, Valerie using shot glasses because you don't keep champagne flutes in a seafood shack. But maybe that's lucky because there are at least twenty celebrants, even the pimply faced fourteen-year-old who buses the tables, and only one bottle, so Clio takes the tiny glass and turns it up.

From the corner of her eye she can see him, out the big plate windows all along the front of the restaurant. Dupree in his produce truck, driving away, this time for good. Even though it's darker than Egypt out that window, even though the willows lining the marsh look as sinister as monsters dragging their low heavy arms, she knows what truck that is that's driving away. Dupree's passenger side tail light has been burned out ever since the night she first met him.

The die is cast. Her fate is assured. There's nothing left for Clio to do but watch that one little yellow square grow smaller and smaller in the distance and drink herself up a cup of foam. All the while thinking that this isn't even remotely how she thought champagne would taste.

****

She's not all that steady on the bike at night. A while back the beach council put in big

216

streetlights, the kind that curve and hang out over the road, so it's not like she can't see and there isn't much traffic either, but Cully normally only peddles among the same three or four places: the library, the grocery, the gallery, the bank. Her bike's old school, with one of those wire baskets on the front like Angela Lansbury had in that murder show. Cully never understood why Angela didn't move out of that little Maine town. Hell, it didn't look any bigger than Elliott Point but somebody got killed there every damn week.

She'd tried to put the painting in the basket at first, but of course it didn't fit. She kept messing with it past the point of reason and ended up tying it to the back fender with a tape measure, the only ropey thing she could find. It's not secure. It shifts and frets her as she negotiates the bike, which is probably why she feels so off balance peddling her way across the bridge. The arch is steep, or at least enough so that she has to stand to push down on the pedals with every pump of her legs. The island just over her shoulder looks bright tonight, she thinks. Studded with car lights and street lights and house lights but the mainland ahead is flat and dark and every time she sits down in the seat and faces forward, Cully's nerve fails her a bit. She's got no business leaving the island on a bike, not with night having fallen like a heavy velvet curtain. If she was going to give this man one of her paintings, she should have done so this afternoon and let him be the one to figure out how to get it home.

And yet she had stood there like a dummy and watched him walk away from her with empty hands.

Cully stands and wills her legs to pump harder. Her heart doesn't like it. It twists and burns and scolds her but just when she's about to give up, she crests the apex of the bridge and starts down. Which should be good news but as it turns out, bridges are a lot like the rest of life– you might think it's the climb that'll kill you but in the end the descent turns out to be the hard part. Cully's bike threatens to get away from her on the basis of sheer momentum, and she rides the brakes the whole way down, cursing out loud as the painting flops and twists against her back tire, each ker-thump reminding her she's come out in the dark, all alone, on a fool's errand.

But she's past the point of no return now. Literally. Once you've crested the bridge it's as hard to go up as it is to go down so Cully finally eases into the seat and lets the bike take charge, expecting to crash against the railing at any minute. Or who knows? Maybe she'll flip clean over the side and land in the intercoastal waterway. At least it's high tide.

But three or four more seconds and, just like that, the road starts to level and she's down. She doesn't stop by braking. She stops by driving the bike straight into a bank of sand. Her hands are shaking as she unknots the measuring tape and loosens the painting. It's another sharp turn down to the pier from this point so she figures she may as well leave the bike by the road and walk from the bank to the dock.

*He can sell the painting after I'm gone,* she thinks, her feet skidding and slipping in the soft sand. *That'll keep him in beer and pinto beans for a few months. A year if he's careful.* She thinks this on the surface of her mind even though on a deeper level she knows he'll never sell the gift she's lugging towards him. Once she's gone he'll probably sink it in the bay or burn it on the pier, something dramatic like that. Something pointless. Yeah, she's a fool going to see a fool on a fool's errand, no denying any of that, and yet Cully keeps walking, using her phone as a flashlight with one hand and dragging the painting behind her with the other.

The dock is faintly lit, she's relieved to see. It gives her something to aim for in the darkness. Four lights are burnt out among the six poles, but the two left give enough illumination that she can make out the shape of the little hut at the end of the pier. *His life looks horrible to me,* she thinks. *But who am I to say? He may have found peace. This man may have found more peace I ever dreamed of having.*

She steps onto the weathered boards, taking care, for they are warped and uneven, with nails poking up at odd angles and they smell of rot. The lone window in the hut is glowing blue, so he's there. Watching television, or maybe he has a computer. Something rumbles overhead, crossing above her on the bridge. The weight of the speeding vehicle ripples the water. Cully looks up.

An ambulance, its lights flashing. No surprise there. Somebody somewhere is always out getting themselves hurt.

****

A convertible's such a damn cliché. A sign of a certain kind of man who's reached a certain stage in his life but at least they let you look up at the sky. Amy jerks the passenger seat back until it's almost flat and studies the darkness above her. She'd chugged the first shot and the man has gone to get them another. They're parked outside a bar in the middle of nowhere. In fact, if the boondocks had an address, this would be it.

She'd asked him to take her to Shalotte, that much is true, but they blew past the sign to Shalotte twenty minutes ago and she's still not entirely why he took her this far off the island. She's married, he's married, and true, their faces are known around town, but even so. It's just a drink. Are all these precautions really necessary? They'd driven due west another ten miles before he saw this little bar and did a u-turn in the middle of the road to get back to it. Then on top of that he'd insisted they drink in the car. Apparently this is the sort of place that provides whisky to go. He'd told her to sit tight and he'd be right back and so she'd waited, vaguely uneasy in the silence.

He yanks the car door open and she looks at him expectantly. He hands her the glass.

"You're not up for another round?"

"Not quite yet. You passed me."

"I'm just getting going," she says, and lifts the little juice glass to her lips.

"Looks like you were studying the sky pretty hard."

Amy settles back flat and extends a finger. "That's Cygnus."

He slides in beside her and looks up. "Cygnus like a swan?"

"Yeah," she says, surprised that he knows this, although she isn't sure why she's surprised. It's not like she's ever tried to have an intellectual conversation with this man. He probably just thinks of her as Brian's wife. "Exactly. Cygnus like a swan."

"I'm surprised you can find it," he says. "The swan's not exactly the most obvious shape in the sky."

"You're saying I'm dumb?"

"I have no idea if you're dumb or smart. The longer we sit here in the dark, the more it occurs to me that I hardly know you."

Even though she'd been thinking the same thought about him seconds earlier, Amy is hit with an irrational bolt of anger. She raises her neck high enough to chug the second drink, feeling the whisky scrape its way down her throat. "Merry showed me how to find it. She's kind of an astronomer. Her daddy even built her an observation deck up on top of the house."

"Merry. That's your girl?"

She nods. "Only one I have."

He's still nursing his first drink, and even though she rather pointedly slams the little juice glass on the dashboard, he doesn't ask if she's ready for a third. "What's she like?"

*Difficult,* Amy starts to say. *Prickly and fussy over things that don't matter.* But she knows

223

that those same accusations could be made of her, so instead she asks "Got time for a story?"

"I always have time for a story."

"We were driving down here just a couple of weeks ago. Driving on this very road but farther up. You know, after you leave Bennettsville but before you get to Dillion. Batting our way down in that damn minivan loaded to the gills and we'd gotten a late start. Adam -he's the athlete- had just finished his last All Star Game. Finished on a loss."

"Almost everybody does."

Everything anybody has said all day has seemed to piss her off and this is no exception. "What's that supposed to mean?"

"Nothing. You know. Tournaments and stuff. Everybody exits until there's only one team left standing. It's the way the system is set up. Lots of losers. Not a lot of winners."

"I guess so. But the minute he got off the field I got him herded into the van with the others, still wearing his cleats, and we took off. I don't know why I was so determined to get down here that night. I normally don't like driving in the dark."

"Maybe you felt like you'd already been cheated out of the first two weeks of summer."

"That's it," she says, propping her bare feet on the dashboard and waiting for him to object. "That's exactly it," she goes on when it becomes clear he has no plans to object to whatever she does. "So it was past nine when we hit the road and the boys were asleep in the back before we got past Monroe. Merry was riding shotgun and there wasn't any traffic to worry about but somehow I let myself get low on gas."

He makes a whistling noise through his teeth.

"I know. It was stupid. Here we were flying eastward on our last inch of fumes and coming up on the deer-hitting time of the night. I've never killed anything with my car, can you imagine that?"

"An impressive boast for a Carolina girl. Not a dog or a chicken or a possum or even a squirrel?"

"Nothing."

"A turtle?"

"I believe I said nothing. Which, you're right, is quite a claim to make. But that's the night Merry showed me Cygnus. Now, you gotta know Merry to know how unlikely this next part is but all of a sudden I look over and she's pointing into the darkness and she tells me the swan is long and thin with spread wings and she asked if I could see her. I snuck a look up and didn't have a clue."

"So you lied?"

"Well, sure. Merry hardly talks to me anymore about anything so I wasn't going to admit I could barely figure the road through the windshield of the minivan, much less pick out shapes in the stars. I carried on like it was the most magical thing I'd ever seen until she finally gets mad and tells me I'm not even looking in the right direction."

"Where were you when this happened?"

"I told you. Somewhere past Bennettsville. No street lights, hardly any house lights, and by this point it had probably been twenty minutes since we'd even passed another car. Which included cop cars so I was killing it and thinking there had to be a station open up ahead in Dillon. I kept having those moments- you know those moments? When you're riding a road you've driven a thousand times in your life but you look up and, out of nowhere, you don't know where you are? And you feel kind of swimmy and your heart pounds and for a minute you think this must be what death is like- just floating with no sense of time or place?" She glances over at him. "For the record, I do recognize that I sound completely crazy."

"Not a bit. I know that feeling. Suspect everyone does."

"Maybe so. But I was praying just to pass another car, to meet a set of friendly headlights, or even pass a sign by the side of the road telling me how far I was from any semblance of civilization. Churches or cigarette outlets or video game casinos or garden clubs. Any of the above would have been welcome about then. I zoomed through a couple of little towns like this one. Crossroads with a 35mph speed limit and there's maybe a church and a bar...why do they always put a church across the street from a bar? And graveyards of course. Every little southern town has to have a graveyard. That's where we were. Nowhere. And I'm about to have a flop sweat from worrying about the gas and that's when Merry starts up with her stories about Cygnus."

"Stories? What kind of stories?"

The question surprises Amy. "Oh, hell, I don't remember. Merry has a habit of starting out trying to tell you one thing and ending up telling you something else. I guess you're thinking she gets it honest. But this one was about Zeus. You know, the king of Olympus. How he was trying to seduce this beautiful woman named Leda only she'd never give him the time of day."

"Why not? If he was the king, I mean. Sounds like a pretty sweet deal."

"She loved another."

He throws back his drink. "Happens."

"So they say."

"What's that got to do with Cygnus?"

"Zeus turned himself into a swan so he could get close enough to Leda to seduce her."

"Wait a minute. You're saying she'd rather have sex with a swan than a king?" He reaches for the lever and drops his seat as low as hers. "Sounds like a myth alright."

"I might not be remembering that part right. It was late at night, remember, and I was distracted. But I was just trying to explain to you what kind of child Merry is. You asked, remember? She's the kind of girl who looks up at pure darkness, pure nothing, and thinks she can make something of it. Thinks she sees shapes. Tells herself stories about them. Merry imagines that it's possible to understand the world. You know the type."

He sighs. "Sit tight. I'll get us another."

"Good idea," Amy mutters, thinking that Brian's probably walking out of Brewster's at this very moment, seeing her minivan wedged under the bridge. If he's drunk enough to be holding his mistress's hand, this is the point where he'll more than likely drop it. His first thought will be that Amy is merely angry. That she left the minivan as a sign- a way to remind him that at heart he's nothing more than a family man. Most likely he's imagining that she got a girlfriend to help her bring the van there as a big old "screw you" and by now she's merely home sulking. He's probably thinking that he can tiptoe up the stairs with stocking feet and loaded pockets and it won't take any more than a snap of his fingers to win her back.

Or who knows? Perhaps the deeper, darker truth is already beginning to dawn.

The man is back. He hands her another one of those little juice glasses that you get at Walmart, eight for three dollars, and this time he steps into the car without opening the door, swinging one of his long legs over the side and working his way back down into the seat. Amy will never understand why big men like small cars, but they all seem to.

"Do you always drink whisky?" she asks. "Neat, like this?"

He shakes his head and gestures toward the little bar with his full glass. "You'd know why I went that way tonight if you could see the inside of the place."

"Nasty?"

"Makes Brewster's look like an operating room. No way I was risking mixers or even ice cubes and I had a bad feeling about how often they rinsed out the beer taps."

"So that's why you insisted I stay out here?"

"I suspected from the outside it might not be a place for a lady," he says, popping the lever again so that he's totally lying flat beside her. "Okay. So your girl's an astronomer and a handful. Tell me about the boys."

Amy laughs. "At least I know you're not trying to seduce me."

"Why's that? Because I'm not dressed up like a swan?"

She laughs again. Everything seems funny all of a sudden and the whisky hardly even burns anymore. "Any man trying to seduce a woman wouldn't keep asking about her kids."

He doesn't answer. She has the sense she's embarrassed him. After a second or two he says, "You did say that one of them plays baseball."

"Yeah. And the other one doesn't."

"Twins, right?"

"Not identical. Different as day and night. In fact, I'll tell you another story, one that happened on that same night on that same drive. All of a sudden Adam wakes up and says he has to pee. And you've got to know Adam. When he says he has to pee he doesn't mean in five minutes. He means he's about ready to blow. Gets that much from me."

"And you're still not to Dillon."

"I was beginning to think Dillon didn't even exist. But then Merry chimes in and says she has to go too. I told them I'd find a field and pull off the road."

"Can't imagine a pair of city kids liked that."

"You imagine correctly. Merry started talking about snakes and serial killers and I said I'd shine the headlights and then both of them said they weren't going to drop their pants in the middle of a field in the middle of the night and I said to Adam 'drop your pants?' and that's when he confessed he'd said pee but he really meant number two even though I don't know why he'd lie about it. Both of them were hollering that it was a pure emergency."

"The other one didn't wake up? Anthony?'

"Andrew. No, he was either still asleep or had his headsets on."

"When did kids get too good to do their business in a field?"

"I blame myself. Merry won't even eat Duke's."

"Duke's mayonnaise?"

"She makes a big point of saying she prefers Miracle Whip."

"It would appear that you've let the situation get totally out of hand."

"Well, yeah. Me and Brian both. We wanted to give them the good life, but somewhere along the way we turned them into a pair of little ingrates. And I say pair, because Andrew's sweet, in fact this story'll show you just how sweet he can be, but the other two-"

"They expect things."

"Oh God, do they ever."

He rubs his eyes. His voice has gotten sleepy. "So what you're really telling me, pretending to talk about the kids, is why you'll never leave your husband. Why you'll stick with him no matter how many Yankee decorators he bangs beneath the Elliott Island bridge."

It is a remark of such causal cruelty, wedded to such stunning accuracy, that Amy's mouth goes dry. For the first time she wonders, really wonders, why this man has appeared out of nowhere and offered to drive her out into the boondocks just so she can have a couple of drinks in peace and tell him stories about her kids. Stories that have no real point, except that yeah, he's probably right about it all. Nobody fooled anybody here. She chose her husband for his ambition. He chose her for hers. They've built a good life together and that's why there might be some messing around and some long stretches of breakfast table silence, but in the end, bottom line, she won't leave Brian and he won't leave her.

All that said, there's nothing any ruder than someone who takes it upon himself to point out the obvious. Amy looks at this man's profile, barely visible in the darkness, and she starts to remind him that he and his wife have sat at her dinner table, drank her wine and picked her ribs. She starts to point out that her husband most likely made him a rich man today, whether he voted for the proposal or not. Starts to tell him that he needs to treat her with a little more respect, which in this corner of the world pretty much boils down to never telling her things she doesn't want to hear.

But before she can do any of these things, the bells from the church across the street start to chime.

She counts along, more out of habit than anything else, and to her horror it comes to ten. She chugs the last ribbon of whisky from the bottom of the glass and throws it into the weeds lining the parking lot. "We've sat here way too long," she tells him. "I've got to get home."

****

It looks like something a child would do. Worse than something a child would do. Something a drunk child would do. A drunk child who wasn't too smart to begin with and was maybe riding on a train.

Josie suspects the problem is that she's diluted the paint too much. Now it's totally run together in the center of the canvas and turned the color of old putty. Half dry, half not, with no apparent way to fix any of it and all Josie can think is that she never should started yammering to Cully about how she wanted to be an artist. Cully must look at Josie and think she's the biggest idiot who ever lived. Well, second or third biggest. Cully seems to think Clio and Amy are pretty stupid too.

But Clio and Amy have something Josie doesn't have -time- so Josie starts dragging the whole mess over the dunes, trying to figure out a way to make a something out of a nothing. The beach is quiet now. Motionless. Only the moon stands witness to her folly. A wet sail's a heavy thing so her arms are aching after no more than twenty steps and Josie pauses to rest on a clump of sea oats. It would be nice to knock on a door and talk to someone but Clio's little porch light is off and Amy's house is the opposite. Lit up the way kids leave a place when there aren't any parents around to flip switches and scold them about the cost of electricity. They might have invited friends over. Seems she heard some splashing a minute ago and it looks like even Cully has found herself somewhere else to be. Josie saw her on her bicycle just a few minutes ago, the head beam punching a tiny circle of light in the darkness and she had the impression Cully had something tied to back of the bike. Something big and bulky. Her easel and paints, no doubt. She has a fair number of moonlit seascapes in her collection but Josie is still surprised that Cully goes out, at her age, alone in the middle of the night to paint. Cully makes Josie ashamed of her own piddling fears. Maybe her children are right. If she's gone this nutty and lonely her second night in the house, with it not yet even the Fourth of July and plenty of people are still around, how can she be fool enough to imagine she'll make it through to winter?

Josie pushes herself back to her feet and grabs the sail again. She can't very well leave it in the dunes for the rest of them to find in the morning light. One solid yank and the sail responds, seeming to follow her voluntarily now, down the dunes and across the beach, which has narrowed, squeezed in the grip of a high tide. Good. Not as far to walk. Josie drops the sail in the edge of the water.

*Ashes to ashes*, she thinks. *Dust to dust and water to water. We all go back, eventually, to the place from hence we came.*

\*\*\*\*

"You're my first visitor," he says.

Cully nods. This is undoubtedly true.

The room has an odd smell- a combination of beer and brine and turpentine and piss. She doesn't step very far inside the doorframe. The man standing before her - old, but no more than her age- has suffered a great deal, this she knows, and she won't insult him by gagging as she enters his house. The word "visitor" implies a certain contract. A certain level of shared civility between them.

The first room is the only room. A sink in one corner and a toilet in the next, a bed with a tv balanced precariously near the foot of the mattress, and then the other wall is nothing but a door, which the man now steps around to close behind her. Despite herself, Cully shudders. He may as well be clanging shut a prison cell.

What did he call himself earlier today, standing in her studio, drinking her good wine? Ah, yes, "quartermaster," which is a nonsense word, implying epaulets and regattas, not a sad little kingdom made up of a half-rotted dock and a small fleet of rarely-used boats owned by people whose only aim in life is to pretend it's still 1961. The founding members of the yacht club, growing fewer by the year, may have thought they'd done this man a favor by getting him live in this hut rent free, but now, taking it all in, realizing his bathroom and kitchen are one and the same, that he sleeps where he eats and shits where he cooks and that the room does not hold a single chair, she can see it was never truly a favor. Homelessness is a step above this. Homelessness at least has air and hope and light.

"I'd ask you to sit..."the man says, with a half gesture toward the unmade bed. It's either that or the toilet.

Cully shakes her head. "I haven't come for long," she says. "I brought you a painting. Left it out on the dock. The one you admired. It's dried now."

"Dried?"

"I always tell people that waiting for a painting to dry is like weaning a puppy," she says, although she's never said anything so silly in her whole life. It's just that she's nervous now that she's actually here. Coming face to face with what the years have done to this man has humbled her. Made her wonder how she managed to live on, to even thrive, when he so obviously did not. She puts it down to a hardness within her. Almost everyone she knows has commented on it as one point or another, from her grandmother to her granddaughter and a hundred souls in between.

"You brought me a dry painting," he's says slowly, as if he doesn't quite understand what's happening.

"They're like puppies being weaned," she says again, right on the verge of babbling. "Once they're dried they can go to their new homes. I want you to have it. It's the one with the shadow."

He doesn't say anything for a minute but she thinks he's frowning. Her eyes are starting to adjust to the gloom.

"I thought you said they all had a shadow."

"Right," she says. "Maybe I should have said I've brought the painting that you specifically admired today at my house. I call it Women in the Dunes, which is kind of a pretentious name and doesn't even make any sense since there's only one woman in the picture. I'll probably change it but It's the last one- the last one I've done. That should make it count for something, sooner or later."

As she says all this her eyes are continuing to adjust and she finds herself staring at another picture, this one hanging above the bed. The only piece of ornamentation in the room.

It is, of all things, a full-sized portrait of her younger son, framed in gold, as out of place in this shack as a punchbowl on a rocket ship. The image has obviously been blown up from a smaller picture that originally held all three of her children. A picture that was swiped somehow, most likely from her own home. Swiped and edited and then expanded. Two human faces were discarded in a Kinko's trashcan and the one who remained was turned into a blurry image of a sweet-faced boy, about ten, staring off into a future he was not destined to inhabit. Cully has not seen this picture in years. She had almost forgotten it exists.

And yet somehow, here it is, on this wall.

"How in the name of God did you get your hands on that?" she says. She means to sound stern but her voice comes out wobbly.

No matter. His own mind is a thousand miles away. "I was on the zoning board for a while," he says vaguely, looking around the shadowy room. Had some money. Had myself a wife and a fancy car."

"I know. But that was a long time ago. You seemed pretty pleased with yourself."

242

"But you never asked me how I got any of it. Maybe you should have. It's an interesting story."

"If I'd stopped to figure anything I probably would have said your family sold their farm and you came into a percentage of the money. Money will always buy you a certain kind of status, at least in a place like this."

"Okay," he says, draining his beer. "So maybe it's not such an interesting story after all. But yeah, we sold our land and I got my piece. Not a fortune by everybody's standards but a hell of a lot more than I'd ever seen. More than my wife had ever had her hands around, that's for sure."

*So what are you doing here? Living alone and drunk on some rotten pier?* Even as her mind asks them. Cully knows her questions are unfair. If some families had a family tree, the Duprees had a family vine, with shoots splitting off in all directions, popping into more kids than they knew what to do with, kids who grew faster than late summer watermelons. Okay, so they sold the land and split it fifty ways and maybe his piece of the farm didn't come to as much as you'd think. Still, he'd once been a man of some

243

substance in the town and it was hard to see how he'd let it all slip through his fingers.

She pulls herself back to the here and now. "I don't see how any of this explains you having my son's picture hanging here on your wall."

"I stole it."

She shakes her head, even though she is not in the least surprised.

"I didn't come off that farm with a king's ransom," he says, "but it was enough for one of those condos down at the point. My wife had a fancy to live there and I said sure. Didn't particularly want to wake up every morning that far off the ground, but I didn't fight it either. I'd not exactly been the world's best husband as I'm sure you've already begun to guess. So if she wanted to live down at the point, I reasoned I could at least get her that much."

Cully shakes her head again, trying to clear the fog in her mind. After so many years of having no idea what became of him, this is a lot to take in. "You bought a condo at the point?

"Oh, we didn't get that far. But we went on a tour. Saw the model."

"Oh lord. The penthouse model. You went up there with your wife? You met Sheila?"

"I met somebody calling herself a decorator if that's what you mean."

"That's her. Brian's second wife. My replacement. Or maybe I should say my successor since I've got too much pride to think a woman like that could never really replace a woman like me." She stops, looks at him again. "You're telling me you stole a picture of Andrew out of the condo model?"

"It was sitting on a table. She was a decorator so I guess she decided to use your boy for decoration."

Now that's a bit of a gut punch, even after all this time, but Cully has no doubt he's telling her the truth.

"That's exactly the way Sheila thinks," Cully says. "I can see her taking our old family pictures, the ones Brian finally made me put away. I guess I never asked what happened to them after I moved out but no, it doesn't surprise me in the least that Sheila would have carted them down to the condo models and spread them around to make the place look...What's that word she always uses? Homey. She says she has a knack for making places where nobody's living look like somebody's living there."

"Like you said you do in your paintings. Like your shadow."

She swallows. "I don't know. Maybe."

He jerks a thumb toward the portrait on the wall. "That's just part of the picture."

"I know. The original had all three of them in it. It was one of Brian's favorites. Perfectly symmetrical. Merry in the middle and a boy on each side. How did you steal it?"

"Wasn't hard. The ladies were talking about drapes or something. There were photos clustered around everywhere, on every table. I just picked up one of them and stuck it in my pants."

The rest isn't hard to visualize. A man, recently come into some money and married to a woman looking to climb. He's already wracked with guilt when he enters the penthouse model and then there they are,

Andrew's eyes watching him just as they once watched her. Only the man doesn't try to get away from that innocent gaze. He takes the picture with him. Cuts two of the children out of it, has some bargain photo department expand the image of the one who'd been lost. Lost in that way that's nobody's fault and everybody's fault and there must have been a thousand times through the years when he could've turned away from the memory of that one awful night. Could've turned, should've turned, but he didn't. Instead he expanded his guilt until it blurred and hung what was left of it over his bed. Lost his wife in the process. His inheritance, his position in the town- hell, clearly lost most of his sanity.

And now he's standing here, staring her down, after all these years. Mad at her for daring to outlive a memory that had all but killed him.

"A strange thing," he says evenly, as if reading her mind. "It's a strange damn thing that I mourned that boy more than either of his parents."

She whirls around as if she's been slapped. "Don't you dare tell me what I have and have not mourned."

"Well then let's just say at some point you stopped mourning him."

Cully shakes her head. "What you don't know about my life..."

"That night, the one we spent in that corn field. It cost me my marriage."

"Cost me mine too."

"Maybe so, but I always figured you were just fine with that."

"Didn't figure you cried yourself a river either. We've always been pretty good at using each other to bump us along to the next stage of life."

That shuts him up. He goes to the refrigerator. Pulls out two beers and hands one to her.

"Once upon a time," she says, pulling the tab.

"Once upon a time," he echoes, pulling his own tab. He keeps looking around the small room like he's angry and maybe he's got a right to be, her peddling out here thinking she can make peace after all this time by offering up no more reparation than a painting that's not even her best work. Cully gulps her beer.

"Once upon a time," she says, "my own home looked just like this place, only a thousand times over. You want to see a shrine? Hell, for better than a year I wouldn't take his shoes out of the basket by the door. Wouldn't move his jacket off the peg, wouldn't change his sheets or clean out his drawers. Kept buying strawberry roll-ups every week because they were his favorite kind. Neither of the other kids ate them so the boxes just kept stacking up in the pantry, wedged every which way and mashed together, taking up more and more space on the shelf. But I still bought a new box, just like clockwork, every week."

"Listen to what you just said. 'The other kids.' Because that's what you had that I didn't. Other kids."

It's a strange way to phrase it and she starts to tell him that. That his lifetime of grief is curious, and excessive, considering he'd only lost something he'd never fully possessed. But she stops herself from saying this thought out loud. It would be too cruel.

"You think that solves the problem?" She takes a draw of the beer. "You think having two left makes up for the one you lost? Of course you do."

"Didn't see any hint of him today when I was in your house."

She feels woozy all of a sudden. Maybe she should sit down, just perch herself on the end of the rumpled bed and hold on to the television. "That's what I've been trying to tell you. That eventually, after a year or two, my husband made me clear it all out. He said turning a house into a museum wasn't being fair to the others. Don't look at me like that. He was right. We had no choice but to live on."

"And so you threw-"

"Stop yourself right there. Be careful with your choice of verbs. I might have laid to rest a few things out but what did you do? You disappeared. You ran. Dropped off the face of the earth. On one level I can see that's a perfectly logical impulse. Not my decision,

250

but you're welcome to it and that's why you have no idea what I saved or lost or what I left behind. Seems to me as I get older and older that this is the only decision that matters much in life. Why we hold on to some things and let go of others and none of us have the right to stand in judgment of another's choices. Hell, rich or poor, it's all the same in the end. We only have two hands. When the day of reckoning finally comes, a prince can't claim possession to any more than a pauper."

There's a long ugly silence and then he gives her a slow silent clap. "Now there's a real nice speech and not the first one I've heard you give. Not even the first one I've heard you give today. That's the thing I always admired most about you, girl. The way that somehow you always managed to sound right even when you were wrong. In fact, the dead wronger you were about something the longer and the prettier the speeches seemed to get."

"Fuck you."

"Beg your pardon?"

"You never knew me at all," Cully says. She takes the two steps necessary to get to the refrigerator, gives the rusty handle a yank so that she can get a second beer. Getting drunk isn't her best move. Not in the middle of the night on an abandoned pier with nothing but an angry shredded man to help get her back up if she falls. When she falls is more like it, since getting the bike back across the bridge is going to be a dicey proposition under the best of circumstances and yet...and yet she is thirsty. Not just thirsty for a frothy gold liquid releasing cold bubbles on her tongue but thirsty for the pure alcohol. Thirsty for the nectar of forgetting.

She takes a quick chug and looks at the blurry picture. "You know what I kept longer than anything? His silly little Walmart beach towel. I kept imagining it still had his scent on it. You know, that clean salty little boy smell. Or maybe you don't know." Another drag, longer than the first. "It got stolen when I moved down here twenty years ago. Not that anybody was particularly trying to steal a faded old beach towel with the Teenage Ninja Turtles. It just happened to be wrapped around my mother-in-law's silver.

The boys who up and robbed me. They wanted the tea set so they took the towel too."

She cries a bit now. Lets out a sob, along with the tears and it's on her so fast that she can't do much but stand in the center of his floor, shaking and making little animal noises. The sudden change in her demeanor softens the man standing before her. He makes a move as if to pat her shoulder but the gesture dies in mid-air. It's like he's nursed his private pain for so long that he's loathe to share it, even with her. He pulls back mid-comfort and asks a nothing sort of question. "Who'd you say robbed you?"

"Oh hell, who always robs you? People I thought were worse off than I was. People I was half looking down on and half trying to help. Here's the thing. They knew what they had all at once with the engagement ring and the silver. Even my stupid music machine. But that towel. It was all thin and cheap and faded and nobody can name the Ninja Turtles anymore."

"Leonardo, Michelangelo, Raphael and...and Donatello."

"Well all right then. There you go. That's a surprise. You coming up with Donatello is maybe the most unexpected thing that's happened today but okay, good for you. Maybe I should have said that hardly anybody can name all the Ninja Turtles anymore and how the hell would you ... but it doesn't matter. We were talking about the beach towel. Those kids, those thugs, they never realized that towel was the most valuable thing they took from me that night. They probably just pitched it out by the side of the road, somewhere between Bennettsville and Dillon."

\*\*\*\*

Anybody who says you can't go back in time is a fool. A fool, or else they've never been to the beach because Amy feels twenty all over again as the convertible rips across the bridge, her hair blowing wild in all directions. She can hardly see the man who's driving, which is probably for the best. It means she isn't tempted to even try and read the expression on his face. She was hurt, and mad, and drunk and it didn't take long and it didn't mean anything and he's got a wife somewhere so she's pretty sure he won't tell. No one will ever have to know that she's just paid Brian back tit for tat with a man who, by his own admission, in the final analysis of things is little more than a stranger.

Neither one of them has said a word since they pulled out of that corn field. Convertibles are convenient that way. The roar of the wind is so loud it relieves you of the burden of conversation. The man driving the car is already regretting the last two hours of his life. She can tell this without even looking at him, that his guilt will always outweigh hers and that he's trying to calculate, as they zoom toward the sparkling lights of Elliott, just what he owes her and in what form it should be paid.

They turn off the main road, then turn again and again and finally once more, until they roll up to the gates of her house. She reaches up to press a button that isn't there-it's attached to the visor of her minivan, which is still parked outside of Brewster's.

She's going to have a hell of a lot of explaining to do at breakfast tomorrow.

She hops out of his car and walks over to manually press in the code to open the gates. Their oldest child's birthday. She uses it as the code for everything. Which means this man, when he said she'd never leave her husband, was probably right. She thinks like a mother now. What do those stupid cups you buy at souvenir stands say? That mothers stop being the picture. At some point along the path they become nothing but the frame. Good mothers know this. Good mothers don't fight it. Amy's got no life beyond the life that sustains her children and pretending anything is just a waste of time.

The gates swing open. The man zooms through before she can stop him from coming in and, after a moment's hesitation, Amy follows on foot. There are no other cars parked under the house, not the minivan or Brian's beamer.

"Go on," she yells to him. "I'm home. I'm safe. Your duty as a gentleman ends here."

"I'll wait until you get up," he says and she shrugs. This is Elliott. It's not like a woman's going to get raped or mugged in her own driveway. But the headlights of his car do make it easier for her to make her way up the stairs to the landing. She looks back and nods emphatically when she reaches the door, but the car stays still as death and she hopes, briefly, that he isn't going to read more into this strange and random night than necessary and turn a temporary mistake into a permanent problem. She signals again, this time in that way that's meant to wave someone on and puts the key in the door.

It swings open into light and silence. The kids have at some point come downstairs and eaten. This much she can tell by the open pizza box on the counter, with a single slice left inside, the cheese cold and congealing on the surface of the dough. Empty cups are scattered along the counter, along with three of Merry's Diet Coke cans. Collectively they probably contain enough acid to gnaw clean through the lining of her daughter's stomach and all this is another thing she's got to face sooner or later. How Merry's practically stopped eating in the last month or two, how she keeps saying she's fat even though she's skinny, how she does strange things like counting grapes and watering down orange juice, how she all but lives on Diet Coke.

*My world's falling apart,* Amy thinks. But on the drive back she'd already decided that tonight was going to be the bottom she would hit and bounce off of. She can use the momentum of this mistake to change direction, to get purpose and energy back in her step. After all, she's got the best house on the beach, three more or less perfect kids and a probably salvageable marriage. Starting first thing tomorrow, she will stop sniveling and start pulling it all together.

Amy lays her keys gently on the counter and starts upstairs. She gets to the twins' room first. Opens the door and finds Adam asleep inside, curled on top of his bedspread. Andrew isn't in his bed, but then he's always been the true night owl. She approaches the lower bunk carefully and pulls a cover up around her son's shoulders. The sight of his face -angelic, like sleeping children so often are- presents her with her first stab of genuine remorse. The first of many, she suspects. Brian has broken their marriage vows a hundred times. She, only once. It's not logical. There's no math to it. And yet fathers are held to one standard and mothers to something else again. Her one slip cancels out his one hundred. Hits the reset button and brings them both back to the point where they must start again.

She closes the door quietly and tiptoes a dozen steps to the next level, the one that holds Merry and her eternal discontent. Amy doesn't have to wonder if her daughter is still awake. She can hear the pulsations of music through the door. She knocks and waits, not surprised Merry can't hear her over the screams of Blondie, and then pushes it open.

Merry is also on the bed but not in the bed. She looks up with some surprise at the force of her mother's entrance and then reaches over to turn down the music.

"Everything okay?"

"I was about to ask you the same thing. Where's Andrew?"

"In bed."

"No. Adam is but not Andrew."

Merry frowns. "Last time I saw him, he was on the star deck."

"Star deck?"

"Oh, you know, Mom. That's what Daddy calls what you call the observation deck."

Something cold runs through Amy. A knowledge not born of this world. That certainty mothers have when they know, on a cellular level, that their child is in trouble.

"What the hell was Andrew doing on the observation deck?"

Merry is fully sitting up now. She seems to have caught the mood of her mother, seems to have read the sudden flash of panic across her face. "I don't know. I guess he came up to talk to me. Oh yeah. He'd just climbed up to say they'd left me the last slice of pizza." When her mother doesn't say anything, she grows defensive. "I didn't eat, I left it for the boys and he knows I go up there whenever you and Daddy have meetings and leave us alone. So he climbed up and he told me -"

She stops here.

Amy's heart is pounding. "What? What did he tell you?"

"That he was going swimming."

"Swimming? At night? In the ocean?"

"I don't know."

"He told you he was going swimming by himself and you didn't stop him? Didn't you even ask where?"

Merry hesitates. "He wouldn't have bothered telling me if it was just the pool."

"Jesus Christ," Amy says, already out the door and descending the stairs, two at a time. "I left you in charge and you let this happen? It's after midnight. And he's out there by himself?"

"I told him to be careful," Merry calls after her. "Come on, Mom, you know Andrew wouldn't do anything stupid. He's the good one."

****

"You had your other children," he says flatly. "And now you have grandchildren. A mess of them."

She nods. It's a small town. No point in anyone denying anything. "Mia was born," she says. "And then Derek. Alex, Lucy, and finally, trailing along at the very end, here comes Amy Jo. She's the only one who's ever been remotely like me but I promise...I love each one of them with all my heart. But a hundred children can't fill the shape of the one you lost."

Even as she's speaking, making one last stab at explaining her life to him, she knows they're through with this. She's growing impatient and there's something beneath the impatience, a type of skittery electric anxiety. The man standing before her is no longer the one she once knew. God knows what he's told himself all these years about that one particular night but it's clear that at some point he and reality parted ways and it's probably too late in the day to reintroduce them. He has spent decades convincing himself he is the one and only person responsible and there's an arrogance to his suffering. He's turned himself into a character. Clint Eastwood would play him in the movie, or maybe Ed Harris, and he's looking at her defiantly as he tosses his empty beer bottle toward the trash can in the corner.

It misses. The bottle rolls across the cracked vinyl floor, ending up under a bed, where the soft clink of glass suggests it's found one of its long lost brothers.

"Oh God, please stop this," she says. "You blame yourself? Well, guess what, so do I. So did Brian. So did Merry. Adam- he was his twin. Kept saying he should have known. Hell, even Sheila had to go to a psychiatrist and get herself some drugs. And you think you're so special? Because you've decided to dash your life against this particular rock, year after year, until you finally broke it? Well, good for you. But believe me, on this particular point, there's plenty of pain to go around."


****

Amy runs blindly across the sand. From the deck, Merry is yelling after her. Lights turn on from somewhere. Car lights, illuminating the beach and part of her mind realizes that the man's still here, that he never left. He is sitting at the end of her drive, waiting for something else to happen, almost as if he had an instinct. Almost as if he knew people always pay for pleasure, especially people like them. He hits his high beams just as Amy stumbles into the surf.

She doesn't even quite know what she's looking for. Words are coming back to her in pieces. Scraps of conversation, something the twins were talking about over breakfast. Adam teasing Andrew like he so often does. Being a natural athlete gives him a sort of power in Boy World, something he can lord over his quieter, shyer brother, because life knows what to do with boys like Adam. Society will always have a slot to slide a strong bold boy into, so that he pops into place with a satisfying little click, but, God knows, the world has no place for the likes of Andrew. A boy who was born an artist. Who draws on napkins in restaurants while waiting for his food, who remembers random things he read in books and frets about them later. The first time Amy took the twins home to show them off, Mama Jo had taken Andrew in her arms and said "He's an angel." Amy had beamed and then her grandmother had added, almost casually "You'll never raise him."

A beat of silence had followed in which everyone struggled to sort out her meaning and then everyone had rushed to fill the void the old woman's words had created. Amy's mother swooping in, useful and solid for once, scooping the baby from her own mother's arms and murmuring something about the onset of dementia. Her dad had picked up Adam and herded Merry out into the yard, promising her a game of catch. Which would be quite a trick since Amy had never known her father to own a ball.

"She doesn't know what she's saying," Amy's mother had said. "She's gone to the happy place, the Elysian fields."

Maybe so, but Amy had never been able to fully forget the words of her grandmother. The woman who had fed her and housed her whenever her no-good parents had gone on benders, the one who had found a way to always get a bookish girl to the bookmobile, every single week in the summer, the one who'd convinced her that she was special. Destined for way more than this dirt road. Mama Jo had never been wrong about anything before. Why would she be wrong about this?

The coldness of the water stings Amy, makes shudders run up and down her back. She pushes forward, even though she knows it's hopeless. *You're just a big chicken,* that's what Adam had told Andrew at breakfast. *You don't know how to jump or tackle or aim or catch and you won't even swim by yourself unless Mom's watching.* He'd spit it all out, one insult after another, and Amy had shaken her head and said "Adam," just like she always does. Warning the strong one to back off the weak one but all the time distracted because Merry wasn't eating and Merry doesn't eat any more and Brian slept on the couch again the night before and there's always something, isn't there? There's always a reason why the momentarily urgent runs roughshod over the long-term important and we let ourselves become distracted. We miss those slippery moments when heaven opens and we might have pulled meaning and glory out of our own lives. The door opens just a moment, then it closes. The tiniest of flashes, and the opportunity has gone.

But even in her distraction, Amy had seen enough to know that Adam's taunts had made Andrew flush. He'd been drawing as usual, just a pencil on the back of a box of cereal. Tracing Tony the Tiger. It was a compulsion with her younger son, this need to see a whole world in the smallest of details, but, despite Andrew's specialness, or maybe because of it, his brother's opinion matters to him way too much. It's the horror of being twins. Most people are haunted by their unlived lives, their shadow selves, but twins see the road not taken spooling out right there in front of them.

*Chicken, chicken,* Adam had said. *Afraid of everything. Maybe you're really a girl.*

Her arms have gone numb. They may as well have left her body. Her limbs belong to someone else. Her feet have lost all contact with the sand long ago and it's impossible to find a child in an ocean. Impossible to pull a single beating heart out of all this darkness and yet she continues to search, even though she can feel the world of the shore closing in behind her. The lights are brighter now -has the man managed to drive all the way onto the beach?- and there are noises. A high shrill voice, no doubt Merry, still screaming, begging her to turn back but there are other sounds too.

Sirens, getting closer. Trying to tell her that she's already lost him. That she made a mistake, huge and irreversible, when she let that man, that stranger in his grey convertible, pull off the road into a clump of cornstalks and reach for her. She'd reached back and now her baby, the sweetest and best work of her life, is lost somewhere in this endless ocean.

All Amy can do is dive. Time after time, even after she knows it's hopeless. Even after one of the ambulances makes its slow bumpy way over the dune and onto the sand and the wall of people start coming in after her. Advancing in lockstep, all of them imploring her to turn back, shouting "no" each time she plunges back into the surf.

And yet she continues to dive, even though each time she comes up with arms that hold nothing but water.

****

Of all the people who could catch her bending over the toilet throwing up, it has to be Jeanne. They had saved the champagne until almost all the customers were gone. Only a handful of regulars, the kind of people who come to the Spanish Moss often enough that they may as well be staff. So when the queasiness rises Clio feels perfectly justified in going into the customer bathroom to do her business.

Even if her business is puking her guts out. The minute she makes it behind the blue door with its dusty seashell wreath, she's swept with a wave of dizziness. Nausea forces her to her knees and if there was any justice in the universe, she'd have some privacy in this misery. She would've heaved, then stopped and cried, wiping her tears on a scrap of toilet paper, then heaved again and then she would had made a solemn vow to herself. That this would be the last time in her life that she would ever puke. That this would be the last time she would find herself

on a cold vinyl floor, all alone and ashamed-
for nothing is as shameful and lonely as
puking, especially if you're draped over the
toilet with a rich woman's ring sliding
around on your finger, especially if you've
been brought this low on the proudest day of
your life.

If there was any justice in the universe her
shame would have gone unnoticed. But of
course we all know there isn't, so Clio
emerges from her stall to find Jeanne in the
bathroom, leaning against the stucco wall, a
pensive frown on her face.

"You're sick," she says. One can always
count on Jeanne to state the obvious.

"It's the champagne," Clio says, fighting the
urge to grip the counter, willing herself to
walk purposefully to the sink where she can
wash her hands and splash her face. "I'm
not used to it."

"Hell, girl, you had maybe what? Half an
ounce, most of it bubbles? And I've seen you
chug a six pack of Pabst without blinking."

Clio stares down into the sink. The water is
swirling above the drain, the circular motion
catching her off guard and for a minute she

270

thinks she might be sick again. Right here, in front of the mirror and Jeanne. But she pulls herself together and lets fly with nothing more incriminating than a burp.

"Sorry," she says. "Sorry. I guess I let my nerves get the best of me. It's been a big night."

"Damn, girl," says Jeanne, the one who can figure 12% on a ten-top without a pad or a calculator. The one who's smarter than she looks, smarter than Clio if the truth be told because she sniffs it all out at a glance, standing there with her arms folded across her chest, the frown on her face slowly changing to a little smile.

"Damn, girl," she says again. "I believe your mama-in-law needs to forget the showers and the parties and the wedding dress shopping in Atlanta. We're going to have to get your ass married as soon as possible, aren't we?"

****

He stands up straight, pulls himself together for the moment of her departure. "Thank you for the gift of the picture," he says. "I'll honor it. And I'll honor your story too. You didn't have to come here and tell me anything. Not after this much time has passed."

"I hope I was right to say it," she says, pausing in the door. "Seems I owed you that much. It might...it might be a blessing to you in the days to come."

"You'll get back to your cottage all right," he says. It's half question and half statement. Either way, there's nothing for her to do but nod and use her shoulder push open the door.

"Be careful," he says.

"Too late for that," she says, stepping out onto the pier. As the door closes behind her, she thinks she hears him laugh.


\*\*\*\*


Brian was the one who finally pulled her out. Others had tried. A neighbor got there first.

Well intentioned, pleading, but she managed to get enough of an arm free from the water to take a feeble swing at him and then the EMT guy came staggering through the surf to try his hand at the task. Twenty years younger and eighty pounds heavier than Amy but she was fueled by panic and she'd slipped out of his grip, pushing back against his chest and yelling "no," even though each time she opened her mouth to scream all she pulled in was more salt water.

Brian didn't even attempt to overcome the strength of a panicking mother. He knew better. He broke her with words.

"Darling," he says. "Darling girl. Come back to the house with me. He isn't out here in this ocean. Never was. They found him in the pool."

She stops then. Lets herself go limp. She knows without thinking about it what must have happened. Merry hiding. Adam taunting. His father out drinking champagne with a decorator, his mother out chugging whisky with the biggest mistake of her life. The mistake she can't seem to stop making. Andrew was so sensitive he could feel the vibrations of other people's suffering like some psychics swear they can predict earthquakes or tornados. It's a curse to care that much and so her baby, her youngest, the one who held back even on the day he was born and let his brother go first, had climbed up to the observation deck alone, after he knew Merry had gone back down to her room.

Maybe he had no intention of trying to jump into the pool when he first went up there. Maybe it was a notion he'd seized on a whim or maybe he'd been thinking all along that a feat like this, falling fifty feet into a bright blue stamp of water, would impress them. Would make his daddy prouder than any drawing ever could and his sister sit up and take notice and his mother laugh with pleasure at his wild ways. At the very least it would shut his brother up. Or maybe he had merely still failed to understand what she'd said about life insurance. Most likely he'd thought what the young always think. That no matter what they do, no matter how far or fast they fall, it simply isn't possible for a child to die.

Either way, Amy lets Brian take her, for the last time, into his arms. This is what will break them and they both know that. Not what she did in that car or what he did on a lounge chair, but this ocean of pain and guilt they both seem to be lost in. And yet, and yet...a sliver of grace runs between the mother and the father in this moment, and with the knowledge that it is all completely over, it is easy to be kind. He reaches for her and she reaches back. He has come into this water to save something. He must save something. His sanity depends on it, so she lets him save her.

Later she will find it almost impossible to remember how she got from the ocean back to the house. Our minds are kind. They rewrite our lives even as we are living them, editing out the parts that are too painful to accept. In the months and years to follow, Amy will recall only snippets of the next few hours. The way she looks up at one point, her eyes blurred from so much time open in the salt water, her vision strange and distorted, and she will see her grand house alit from every angle, each deck and balcony blazing, as if she and her husband are hosting a party. A bruise on her knee will stand silent witness to the fact that, despite the fact her husband was guiding her to the point of almost carrying her, she must have tripped on the familiar stairs.

She was hustled past the scene by the pool. The man was there. The one who'd gotten her drunk- or, more fairly, the one who had sat and listened while she got herself drunk. The man who'd taken her in a corn field- or, more fairly, who had laid back and allowed her to straddle him. The one who'd whispered "careful, careful" the whole time they'd done that careless thing. The man who'd stayed in his car in the driveway, his headlights illuminating the price they'd both pay for the rest of their lives, the man who'd followed her as she'd run from the house to the beach but who had sensed, even then, the total truth of what had happened. He had turned back toward the house even as she had continued to run toward the water and he had been the one who dove into their family pool and pulled Andrew's lifeless body to the surface of the water. He had stayed just there, still bent over the small still shape as her husband nudged her past the sight of the stretcher, the gurney, the paramedics and all the neighbors clustered around.

The whole island had come, but it would seem that they had come merely to witness, too late to help. They turned like a choir, like a Greek chorus, and watched Amy and Brian lead the processional across the patio toward a pair of open doors. On the other side of those doors there were blankets and glasses of water. Concerned murmurs and the warm, living body of Adam, pushed toward his mother as if from some great distance. The two of them had been the only two people in the room not sobbing. They looked at each other for a minute, locking eyes, nodding in silent agreement that they would collectively carry this piece of the memory as long as they lived and then they were pulled apart by the same sea of neighbors who had tossed them together.

Amy was laid flat on her couch. A doctor stepped forward. Another neighbor, and it would occur to her later that he was something like a retired podiatrist or chiropractor. Hell, maybe even a veterinarian but the important thing in the moment was that he carried oblivion in his hand. A needle, a pill, she didn't care. There was nothing left to do but lie back and close her eyes.

****

It's a whole different group of people on the beach this late at night. Locals mostly, people who wait for the tourists to head out to the restaurants and bars and putt putts, and they carry flashlights. Cully watches the yellow circles dotting the beach, as her neighbors roam between the dunes to the surf and back again. Walking their dogs. Getting their ten thousand steps. Or maybe just putting a period at the end of the day as they make their slow steady progress along the water.

Turns out that after all her worrying, she and the bike had made it back across the bridge without much trouble. It was late when she walked through her front door but all day long she's made it a point to notice the passage of each hour, to honor the date and what it means. She still had plenty of time to take a shower and put on her best dress, to pour the final glass of wine from the good cabernet. She had shaken the last drop free of the lip, and stood feeling the shape of the empty bottle in her hands, still heavy even though the liquid within it had finally run out. There were swirls in the glass around the neck and the label showed an etching of a chateau somewhere, lovingly rendered, the name unpronounceable and French. It seemed a shame to just throw the bottle into recycling and for a moment she considered writing a note and slipping it inside, taking it out into the ocean and letting it loose in the water. But that seemed overly dramatic and besides, she couldn't think of anything to write on the note. In the end she just took the bottle over to the recycling bin and laid it, very gently, on top of yesterday's newspaper. Maybe it's best to let it be carried out, crushed into a different shape, formed to suit a brand-new purpose.

By the time she leaves the house, the water is starting to recede. She feels fine and ready as she wades in hip deep and drops her butt down hard into her favorite beach chair, thinking that she can't even imagine a day any better than this one. In fact, Cully decides this may have been the most beautiful day of the whole year. The waves splash almost as high as her chest and she leans her head back, letting the water seep into her hair.

"This September I would be 82," she thinks. A silly thought, a random thought, because in her failing heart she knows Josie's right. Cully may be 81 in the literal sense but she's also 59 and 37 and 22 and every other age she's ever been too. The ghosts of her former selves still live inside of her, pulling her back into her past at the same time she's breaking free from it, but there's no way to explain this to a young woman. Earlier today the others had only gazed upon her splotched and creaky body with fear, like they were thinking maybe old age is contagious and if they sat too close to her they might catch it. Not a one of them would've believed it if she'd tried to tell them that the longer she's lived the more she has seen that the passing of time can be a woman's best friend. Each hour gives at least as much as it takes. And in fact, when she had looked at them, trembling with the fearful power of their youth, she had felt more wistful than envious.

Because all day long today it was Cully who had seen and savored the things the others had been too busy to notice. The way the last rays of the sun hit the water, the thin scrape of pink clouds across a blue sky. Or like now. An old man with a puppy, and then, from the other direction, a young boy comes leading an ancient hound. He seems a nice child. He walks slowly to accommodate the halting gait of the dog and the two of them pause right in front of her, stopping just at the edge of a tide pool where the boy bends to release the dog. It's hard to see his face in the darkness but it seems that he glances toward Cully guiltily as he does this. Unleashed dogs have been illegal on this beach for years, but she waves her hand, telling him to go ahead and let the beast free. Who is she to deny this gray-snouted creature his final swim of a perfect day?

*Good dog,* she thinks. *Good boy. Strike straight out and don't be timid. Paddle on to Cuba. To the coast of Africa, to China. The world belongs to shaggy old animals like us. Those of who have survived so much they have nothing left to fear and nothing left to lose. Those who know how to experience an entire lifetime in the span of a single day.*

Because if you live your life right, all the best stuff comes at the very end.

\*\*\*\*

She must have fallen asleep on the futon. Must have been dreaming about things being pulled out to sea because when Josie wakes up, the first thing she thinks about is the sail. How she was wrong to give up on it so fast.

It's midnight, maybe later. High tide has come and gone but as she slip-slides her way over the dune she sees that the sail is still there. The water must have caught it and pulled it but it didn't take it all the way out. Josie wades into the surf, the bottom of her nightgown becoming more drenched with every step. She doesn't care. The water feels soft, warm, nearly embryonic, and as Josie lifts the sail from the foam she can see that the picture she tried to paint isn't totally gone. There are shadows on the canvas. Smears. Color and shape, and a sense of movement.

*Monet,* she thinks. *Monet in the rain.*

Back over the dunes she goes, panting and cursing, with her damp nightgown clinging to her legs and cockleburs jabbing her bare feet. She runs inside the house and grabs her switchblade off the kitchen counter. The one she used last night to cut open the cardboard boxes holding her plates and pillows and shoes. Things she once thought might help her to begin again, even if she's already beginning to see that she doesn't need any of that stuff. And then she returns to the beach, holding the knife out in front of her with one hand and a bucket of paint with the other. Slices a healthy section of the sail free and repeats the experiment. Two more wild floods of house paint across the wet fabric and then once again into the water she goes, pulling the sail behind her.

She stands and waits. Counts to sixty. Amy's house is so lit up that Josie thinks it looks like a space ship. Everybody on the beach seems to be there. Cars pulled off the road and into the sand from all directions. Cars that must have been driven recklessly and stopped fast, their brakes slammed in a panic. Two convertibles are parked side to side, along with a fire truck sitting hopelessly by. Why do they always send a fire truck? Three ambulances wait, their sirens cut to silence, but their orange lights still spinning. Whatever emergency they once might have anticipated has passed.

Josie swishes the cloth through the water. The moon dangles low and she has a fleeting impression that something else is out there hovering beyond the sandbar. Something white and still, caught just beneath the surface of the water. Another piece of canvas, perhaps? It seems unlikely. But there have to be abandoned sails all up and down the beach, Savannah to Norfolk, just waiting for her to purchase them for a song.

*If people will buy seascapes painted on old sails,* she thinks, *then they will surely buy seascapes painted on old sails and then soaked in the ocean itself.* She can tell them that the water made the art, not her, which is a little bit true and a little bit bullshit, but a little bit of truth blurred with a little bit of bullshit seems to be the precise version of reality that most people are prepared to accept.

She's lost count but she says "sixty" anyway. Says it out loud and then crouches down to see what she has. The first piece had floated for hours, being pulled out to sea while she was dreaming and that could be part of her magic, part of her sales pitch. That it was the ocean that worked the canvas while the artist merely dreamed. Yeah, that's good. Now that she's had a moment to consider it, Josie can practically hear a chorus of a hundred cash registers chiming like church bells.

Ok, so right now, granted, her so-called art is a bit of a mess. Wet paint on a wet sail adds up to nothing, but as Josie runs the rough cloth through her hands, a smile spontaneously comes to her lips. She can see a smudge taking shape and it would seem that she's one of the lucky ones, after all. This ocean has given her a whole new life. All she has to do is find the guts to live it.

\*\*\*\*

Amy doesn't go to the hospital. Everyone says she should. But she fights herself to a seated position and pushes aside the useless blankets. They've piled them on her in an effort to stop the trembling but she knows this is the kind of cold no blanket will ever take away.

Bile rises in her throat, then falls. She flops and struggles her way to the edge of the couch, dimly aware that the drugs coursing through her body are strong. She should know all these people in her living room but she can't seem to recall a single name. She looks over at the kitchen counter and can see that, even though it's the middle of the night, the church lady casseroles have already begun to arrive. This is the south, after all. The land of good intentions and empty gestures. People keep casseroles frozen at the ready just in case some slut of a woman manages to let her little boy drown. She remembers what her daddy used to say about the way God's people always seemed to love trouble. How they'd show up before the blood had even dried on the linoleum, their eyes gleaming with excitement and their arms bearing pyrex dishes full of tuna and noodles. "Show a good Christian woman a tragedy," he'd say "and her first thought is to pour a can of Campbell's cream of mushroom soup right on top of it."

She laughs then, remembering her daddy. The laugh comes out like a bark, thank god. A half-strangled cry for help. People emerge from every corner of the room and begin to move toward her. Some of them think she is choking. They hold out towels and glasses of water and Bibles, none of which is remotely what she needs. She looks around the circle of faces but she doesn't see the man who pulled Andrew from the pool, nor does she see the one who pulled her from the ocean. Doesn't see Adam and when she manages to croak out his name someone tells her he's been taken away. He'll be sleeping at a neighbor's tonight. Somewhere safe, they say. He shouldn't stand witness to any more this. Shouldn't have seen what he's seen so far.

Merry has no business being here either but no one seems to have thought of that. The girl is sitting directly opposite her mother, her knees pulled up to her chest. She'd lifted her head when Amy first began to make her animal sounds, her eyes wide and searching.

Amy looks back, trying to send her daughter the message that, despite what she might have said in her fury, none of this is the girl's fault. Because it occurs to her now that the last words she said to Merry as she's left for Brewster's this afternoon were something awful like "You're in charge," or "watch the boys." Words that meant nothing at the time, just the sort of throwaway line you toss to your oldest on the way out the door. Amy can't live with the thought that she might have casually said something that will forever be burned into the girl's soul.

Merry stands, moves towards her mother. Cuts through the crowd of people trying to help.

"I want to go up," Amy says and everyone nods. They think she means go up to her bedroom. A good idea, they murmur. She should try to sleep.

Only Merry understands. She takes her mother's arm. Too young to be the one doing this, Amy thinks, but she lets her daughter lead her. They climb the first flight of stairs, then the second. he people below are chirping like little birds and saying they will be up in a minute too. They will find towels and sheets and tuck them all in but Merry silences the town below with a single, well-chosen, brutal word and only continues to lead her mother skyward through the house. As the pair of them climb the second set of stairs the murmurs from below become less distinct.

They pause for a moment at the level of the master bedroom. Merry could release her here. Lead her toward the bed. But, as if through an unspoken agreement, the two of them keep climbing all the way to the observation deck perched within the highest eaves of the house. Merry wrests open the door and stands back, letting Amy step first onto the deck.

She doesn't know what she expected. People here too, perhaps, or even crime scene tape but the people gathered in her house don't seem to have realized exactly what happened. They think Andrew went for a late-night swim alone and tired, or hit his head on a ladder, or got a cramp. Only Amy and Merry and Adam understand that the boy, for reasons they will debate silently, within their private hearts for decades to come, climbed to the top level of the house alone, thinking he could jump all the way from the observation deck to the pool. That he entered the water with such force that the air was knocked out of him, that ribs were broken and lungs collapsed.

*Don't tell yourself he died in the water,* Amy thinks. *Tell yourself he died in the air.*

Which hardly matters, not in the light of all that has happened in this horrible and endless day, but Amy stares down at the pool, people still clustered around it, an empty stretcher still waiting, and then pushes back. She sinks into the chaise lounge and looks up at the sky. Merry climbs onto the lounge beside her. Curls her body around her mother's and simply hangs on.

A long silence.

"Look," Amy finally says. "The stars are special tonight."

Merry keeps her face buried in her mother's shoulder. "They're special every night," she says, her voice muffled. "We just don't usually pay attention."

When Amy doesn't answer, she lets go of her and rolls over, so that they are both lying on their backs. Shoulder to shoulder crammed within the confines of the chaise, both staring into the night.

"Where is he?" Amy asks.

"He and Daddy are headed to the hospital, I guess." Merry hesitates. "Or maybe the coroner took him."

"No, I mean, where IS he?"

"I don't know," Merry says, with some urgency, for the crowd of people come to stand witness to their grief, the army of judgment that rises up in every small town when guns are fired and hearts explode and cars collide, have begun to realize that they did not stop on the level of Amy's bedroom. That the mother of the dead boy is not tucked in and oblivious but rather high in the sky and fighting the tranquilizers with every fiber of her body. Below them is the dim beeping of a rising elevator, the soft pad of feet coming up a carpeted series of stairs. This time to sit together and look into the sky will be brief. They will soon be pulled apart and fed casseroles and talked to about Jesus and numbed with more pills so Merry turns to her mother with urgency and whispers "Cygnus. She had twins. Did I tell you that part? "

"She married Zeus..."

"And bore him twins."

"I think I see her." Amy says, pointing into the blackness. "You're telling me you think she's carrying him?"

"Maybe. All I know is that she's flying awful bright tonight."

"Flying bright tonight," Amy repeats, her eyes closing. "Flying away."

****

We meet our destiny on the road we took to avoid it.

Cully read that once, a long time ago. She can't remember where. Probably in the hot concrete parking lot of a Winn Dixie, when she was sitting on the curb gobbling down words, trying to finish one book so she could swap it for another before the bookmobile left. It seems to Cully that she's always been rushing, always hungry for more, and trying to grab it up from all directions. So for once it's nice to sit like this, with nowhere to go and nowhere to be.

*I'm tired of being old,* she thinks. *I'm pretty much tired of being anything.*

Endings are funny. They never hit you quite like you think. She's been counting the days off on her calendar like a child waits for Christmas, saving the pills, using the internet to try and figure the perfect dose, and yet now that the time's finally come, it's just like the message in the wine bottle. She can't quite think of what she wants to say.

She's certainly ready to see him again. At first she had even chased him. She'd hired psychics and mediums and hypnotists, flew to California and Honduras, Jerusalem and Nepal in search of answers. Nothing had worked. There were years in which she drank too much, tried to forget. There were years in which she dreamed too much, afraid that she'd forget. For a long time she'd thought that the pain of outliving her son might actually kill her. It came close. Gnawed its way through her breast and into her chest but then, out of nowhere, came that one particular summer when -with no hope or expectation– she'd started to paint.

And from that point on she always knew exactly where to find him.

He waited for her on every canvas, smudging his way into every landscape, showing her that he'd never really left Elliott Point at all.

The stars are clear tonight, especially considering there's a full moon and Cully chuckles, despite the pressure in her chest. She can't tell if it's nostalgia or angina. She's at the stage of life where joy and pain feel almost exactly alike. *Nothing left to do but breathe into it,* she thinks, settling back one final time. *Take it all in, let it all go.*

And then as Cully watches, as from a great distance, the seascape before her begins to melt. The sky stretches and slides, star by star, light by light, into the whirling foam.

****

There are three different news stations covering the coast and each one takes a slightly different tone toward the tragedy.

The Florence report is clipped, nearly military in its language. The field reporter says that a stronger than average current, aided by the surge of a moon tide, had "dislodged the woman's position." Wilmington merely informs listeners that receding water claimed an elderly resident's body. The Charleston station, drunk on hanging moss and tragic history, is by far the most romantic. It says that a local artist had been picked up in the arms of the sea and carried home.

Everyone claims that words shape reality, and maybe they do, but no matter how you say it, the truth comes down to just a few facts: Cully had been floating in the ocean for hours by the time Dupree found her the next morning. Her flesh had been nibbled by a hundred small mouths and seaweed had snarled in her long gray hair. A lesser man might have cried out, almost screamed, for the overall effect of her slow, incremental drowning had given the woman an otherworldly appearance. Florence,

Wilmington, and Charleston all stood in agreement that what the old man did next was heroic. He charged into the surf, his bad heart pounding, leaving his dog to bark hopelessly on the shore.

A middle of the night drowning meant the local paper had to scramble to meet the deadline, but the woman was somewhat famous, after all, and old enough that her death was not utterly unexpected. Her obituary had already been partially written and the next day it is the headline of the afternoon paper.


Amy Josephine Cully Elliott


Born April 4, 1939 in Clio, SC, Amy Josephine Elliott is best known to many locals as the former wife of Brian Elliott, area restaurateur, hotelier, and developer of the Elliott Point project. Later in life, Mrs. Elliott received statewide recognition for her artwork, which featured an unusual "abstract seascape" technique, partly achieved by being soaked in salt water and partly from being painted on nautical sails.

Working simply under her maiden name of "Cully," Mrs. Elliott became a four-time recipient of the South Carolina Folk Heritage Award in the visual arts category. One of her paintings, September Sunset, hangs in the governor's mansion.

Mrs. Elliott died in the place she loved best. Her body was found by William Dupree, who, by chance, had known Mrs. Elliott in her youth. Mr. Dupree, 83, is being hailed for the extraordinary efforts he undertook in order to retrieve the remains of Mrs. Elliott, which had been carried out to sea. Upon examination by the Horry County Coroner, the cause of death was determined to be heart failure.

Mrs. Elliott is survived by two children, Merry Madison of Charlotte and Adam Elliott of Atlanta, as well as five grandchildren. She was preceded in death by her son Andrew Elliott. Funeral services will be private but a reception celebrating the art and life of Cully will be held Sunday afternoon, July 2, at the Cygnus Gallery in the Elliott Towers Marketplace. The gallery owner, Ms. Sheila Montgomery Elliott, has announced that all paintings by the artist, including a variety of half-finished panels, are available for sale.

****

Even in this allegedly enlightened day and age, certain kinds of work always fall to the daughter.

Adam had declared himself too distraught to face the task of cleaning out his mother's studio and thus, shortly after the services, had retreated back to Atlanta. Merry hadn't particularly wanted the thankless chore of hauling away cans of turpentine and rotted canvas either, much less selling the beach house and dividing the proceeds two ways, but for her entire life she has found it nearly impossible to fight Adam. Give her a couple of weeks to get her feet back under her, she told him. After all, she's in shock too. No one had expected Mom to die, at least not right now, and certainly not from a heart that simply stopped beating. She seemed like the kind who would have gone out in a more dramatic way- plunging from the sky in a parachute accident, murdered by a drifter or maybe spontaneous combustion. Something like that.

Just let me have two weeks, she told her brother. Three, maybe four. Hell, give me until September. It's not like anything's going anywhere. Let this damn summer pass, then I'll drive down from Charlotte and figure out what has to be done.

But for all her complaining, as her car crests the bridge bearing her father's name, part of Merry is glad to be coming back to Elliott Point on her own. She hasn't been here since the funeral and she isn't sure how she feels about driving these streets now. The car blinks, slows and turns by instinct, like it knows the way back better than she does and it's almost a relief that there's no one riding along beside her expecting her to talk. If she wants to cry, or laugh, or drink, or torch the damn place into a heap of ashes, nobody's there to try and stop her.

She started from Charlotte at dawn so it's still morning when she arrives. September has always been her favorite month at the beach. There's an irony that the season ends just when the beach is at its most beautiful. The sky is Crayola blue and the day feels mellow, like a perfectly ripe golden apple and as Merry pulls into the driveway it occurs to her that she will be 59 next month. The exact same age her mother had been when she moved down here. When she had insisted on buying that tiny, rundown cottage in the very shadow of the home her ex-husband still shares with his second wife. When she had returned, as they say, to the scene of the crime. At first it had seemed so perverse, like she was rubbing it all in Brian's face. Not just Andrew's death but her self-imposed poverty, her self-imposed exile and of course her accidental cancer, sandwiched between the two. Her never-ending anger over his decision to develop the point.

"Leave it alone, Mom," Merry had begged at the time. "Let Daddy and Sheila do whatever Daddy and Sheila have to do and let Andrew rest in peace. There are a thousand beaches along the Carolinas. Go find yourself another one. Or if you can't, at least tell Daddy he owes you a condo in the high-rise. You know he'd be happy to let you take your pick and if you were living down at the point, there'd be people around you year round. Lights will come on when you hit the switch. The toilets will flush. That's where sixty-year-old women need to be. There's no need to burrow in right underneath him and Sheila so that you can keep popping up when they're just trying to drink margaritas on the deck, acting like you're some kind of goddamn ghost of summers past."

But her mother had just kept saying that moving back to Elliott had nothing to do with Andrew's death or her failed marriage to Merry's daddy. She kept saying she wanted to buy back the same cottage she'd rented forty years earlier, when she'd first come to the coast to waitress. That this was what she thought of whenever she heard the word "home." The only place that had ever been completely hers and felt completely right.

And then Mama had moved into the damn thing and started to paint and that had been that. Merry had gotten used to it in time. This is Merry's greatest skill as a human being. She can get used to anything in time.

The same oversized key they've always used is still there, badly hidden behind a floppy shutter and as Merry pushes the door open, her throat catches. There's that smell. Salt water and turpentine and Coppertone and booze and childhood. Mom had been right about one thing, Merry thinks, as she walks across the sandy floor of the dimly-lit room. There were certainly no rules here. Nothing you had to keep clean and nothing you had to worry might break. Merry's own kids had loved coming down and had made no bones about the fact they preferred this musty little firetrap to vacationing at their grandfather's mansion next door, even though he had the pool and the game room and big screen and hot tub. But they always claimed it was better at grandma's where you could make your own pancakes out of Bisquick and play music as loud as you wanted. Walk through the door with sand on your feet. Eat watermelons on the porch and throw the scooped out rinds into the dunes.

With a deep breath to steady her nerves, Merry strides straight toward the studio, not even pausing to put down her purse. The front part of the cottage was added on when her mama, to the surprise of everyone in Christendom, all of a sudden began making a little money. When she finally mustered up the gumption to stop being Josie and start being Cully.

The studio is all glass, bought from some company that marketed it as a greenhouse. The panes are curved to intensify the light so that things will grow faster and as a result the glare from the midday sun is so bright that Merry jerks back a bit as she steps into the room. The studio has always been uneasily attached to the original house-twisted oddly, with the doorframe too narrow, and bolted together in a way that leaves it vulnerable to hurricane season leaks.

None of this had seemed to bother Cully. She only cared about having certain angles but then again, artists always do. "The point of view is the point," her mother always said and the studio is just as she left it. Two fine-stemmed glasses are sitting side by side on a table, barely touching. The final drops of wine left in the bottom went acrid weeks ago and it's surprising Sheila missed them in her sweep. Adam said their stepmother was in the studio before Mama had even gone stiff, grabbing up everything that wasn't nailed down. Taking the paint rags and pencil sketches, claiming it was all for the gallery and that Cully's worth was sure to double with her death and then stopping, hearing her own voice, and the way her voice had risen with an unseemly degree of enthusiasm on the word "death."

"I want the best for her," Sheila had finally finished, her voice falling almost to a whisper. "Your mother was a true creative, as fine as any I've ever had the pleasure to represent, and her reputation deserves the chance to grow."

"Which means more money for the two of you in the end," her father had added. "You and your kids. It's what Amy would have wanted."

Merry knows there's no point in resenting her father or snubbing his wife. Adam holds a grudge but then Adam has always been the bristly one, reading more into things than the situation calls for. The problem is really her mother. The problem is always the mother. Daughters know that. Sons don't, so for Adam, the minute Mama had died she had gone from Eccentric to Saint in the blink of an eye, which is one of the reasons he claims he can't bear to help his sister come down here and sell the house.

So it's Merry and Merry alone standing here in the too-bright September sun trying to make sense of it all. The way Mama always seemed to slide through life in stages. The hardscrabble girl who fought her way out of the sticks and swore she'd never look back, even though, as it turns out, she never did anything but. The young mother with three kids, one of whom slipped through her hands and then the way she went all around the world looking for answers until, without warning, the brutal grace of cancer had stepped in and saved her life. Turned her into Mama Jo's Josie, made her an artist in her own right, the last thing any of them would have expected, and it's all kind of surprising and inevitable, and in the end maybe the why of it all doesn't come down to much because Merry knows she needed today. She needs to do this. She didn't know how important it was to say goodbye until she actually crossed the Elliott Island Bridge.

As Merry stands here in the studio, gazing over the tops of the dunes at the blue panel of the sea, she sees that a man is approaching. Old, tall, thin, with a stoop. He looks familiar.

Maybe he's the man...she's almost sure he is. The one who'd found her mother's body. The man who'd pulled her in at some risk to himself, falling in the process, breaking a bone in his hand and yes, the man easing his slow way across the dunes still has one of those soft casts around his wrist. Hard to say what he's doing here today but the least she can do is go out and greet him. Thank him properly, which she really didn't do at the funeral. There had been so many people and she had been in such a fog. He'd introduced himself as Bartholomew Dupree, looked her right in the eye, and said "I'm so sorry."

And all she'd been able to answer was "We all are."


****


"Don't you dare tell me what I've suffered." That's what Cully had said to him the last time they'd talked. She had wiped her eyes and told him how her boy had been an artist. Born to be a real one, not just somebody playing around with sails and salt water like her, and that she'd kept every drawing he'd ever made. Kept them hanging up in that big white house until her husband had finally pulled them off the walls and it had been that singular gesture -not the affairs or the funeral or the high rise on the point- that finally snapped their marriage in half. Her husband had yanked one of Andrew's drawings off the refrigerator where it had been hanging with a magnet for better than two years. A starfish, not even Andrew's best work. A bit childish and clumsy but the last picture he'd ever done, drawn on the longest day of the year. Brian had said "Seriously, Amy, it's time" and crumpled the starfish in his hand.

"You're right," she said and that had been the end. That very day she'd packed and gone back to Charlotte with the two kids she hadn't yet managed to kill and left him to his Yankee decorator.

"It was like rewinding a movie," she told him. "I threw them in the car that night like I should have two years earlier and Merry said-"

"Merry," he'd said.

"Merry," she'd said. "That's the girl. Don't tell me I've never mentioned her name. Not Mary, like the virgin or the little lamb, but Merry spelled like Christmas. And that's a clue, by the way. A clue just in case anybody around here was inclined to go searching for a clue."

He didn't rise to the bait. Not yet, anyway. It had felt so strange to be standing there in his little house with her, Miss Forever High and Mighty, a woman who had always been happy enough to sleep with him but who had made it clear he wasn't fit for much else. At times he had thought that he dreamed her. The hours they'd spent together had been so different from the rest of his life. The colors brighter, the sounds and scents more distinct. He'd have been a different kind of man if she'd married him...but she didn't and he wasn't and that was that. The morning he'd seen her napping on the beach was the first time he'd laid on eyes on her for forty years and yet here she stood, his first and most likely only visitor, the one person who'd stood witness to the best and worst moments of his life.

"There's a starfish picture on your fridge right now," he finally said. "Faded and crumpled, but it's there."

"Well, sure. Yes. Goddamn right. I pulled it out of the trash the minute Brian's back was turned."

It would be the last conversation between them. She likely knew it but he sure hadn't and so he'd repeated every word they'd said a hundred times in his head every day since she died, just as Dupree's feet seem to keep walking him here, to this dune in front of Cully's house. No one knows he makes the long trek across the bridge at least twice a week, except maybe his dog, and Max is good at keeping secrets. Some people might say it's morbid to go back time and again to a place where you found a dead body. But he feels compelled to relive every moment of that day, probing it despite the pain, the way you tongue keeps finding its way to a sore tooth.

First they had been at her house. There had been pictures everywhere. She'd offered him a glass of wine and he, against his better judgment, had accepted. Good wine, even he'd had the sense to know that. She seemed to be treating the whole day like a celebration and she'd offered him a second pour. The people at the Second Baptist AA meeting wouldn't have been glad to see how readily he'd accepted, but the truth is he would have drunk up anything she served him. Drunk it up gladly, stammering and trembling, his eyes darting around that ramshackle cottage- changed but still full of memories. They'd walked around each other more or less, both of them so shocked at finding the other one back like this, standing right in front of them, that neither could think of much to say.

It hadn't been until she came to see him later, dragging that picture, that they finally found the nerve to get down to what they both needed to confess. She'd been so damn uncomfortable that she'd been in and out of his shack in ten minutes and he couldn't say he blamed her. He'd walked her down the pier as she left, making some foolish talk about her being careful on her bike, even though there were a couple of points when she'd all but told him what she was fixing to do. Even if she had said it straight out, he's not sure he would have believed her. Clio had always been dramatic, using a dozen fancy words when a single plain one would do, and he probably would have just assumed she was saying that she was more than ready to die, a sentiment he could completely understand. When they'd come to the end of the rotten boards -both of them shaky, both of them old- he'd just blurted it out.

"I need to hear you say it. For once just flat out say it. You married him because he was rich."

"No."

"No?"

"Maybe partly."

She always had been honest. He liked that about her but he'd lashed back with anger nonetheless.

"Ain't no 'partly' about it. I could build you a sand castle. He could build you the real thing."

She had turned towards him then. No longer shoulder to shoulder. Now face to face. "And I kicked it over, didn't I?"

"Besides," she added, just when he was fixing to say something else mean. "What was I supposed to think after finding a red bra stuck up under the front seat of your pick-up truck?"

That had given him pause. "What the hell are you talking about?"

"The same day Brian asked me to marry him. I went out in the parking lot on my break to think and I climbed into your truck."

"Why'd you do that?"

"Because it smelled like you. Smelled like how I'd been raised, if the truth be told, and I thought it might clear my head. Only that's when I found it. A red bra, balled up and stuck down under the seat."

He'd jerked. "Red" and "Bra" can be ugly words.

Her voice was cold. "Don't act like you don't know what I'm talking about."

"Oh yeah," he'd said. "I remember it all right. Only it was more pink than red and it wasn't under the seat. It was waiting for me on the dashboard."

"I'm not interested in arguing details. What I want to know is, who left it in your truck?"

"How the hell should I know, woman? You just said you did."

"I said I found it. Moved it from the floor to the dashboard to make a point, but it sure wasn't me who'd left it there. I ask you, have you ever known me to have a red bra? Does that even sound like something I would possess?"

He had paused then, weaved a little. The moon had come up while he'd been inside his house watching the Big Bang Theory like he always did this time of night. But now the light hit the water of the bay like a beacon, leading a man toward some truths, throwing others into shadow. "You've always been able to confuse me, Clio, and now you've confused me once again. What exactly are we talking about?"

"You remember Jeannie?"

"Do I remember- what the hell? That little fool from the bar? You think that was her bra?"

"I know it was her bra. What I'm asking is how it got in your truck."

"I don't know."

"You don't know."

He'd hesitated then, knowing she wouldn't leave until he'd give her more. She'd ridden out here at significant effort and even some danger, peddling her way over that bridge and she wasn't going to leave until their exchange was fully finished.

"I'd give your little waitress friend a ride home every once in a while, if by chance she and me wound up in the same honky tonk," he finally said. "If she'd been drinking. And lord knows, she was always drinking."

"On that score, you and me got no room to talk."

"True. True enough. But Jeannie was always looking around. There's a certain type of female, you know that as good as me. She's still in the bars at midnight, just sitting there fiddling with her compact, as they're turning on the lights and calling last call. Trying to find some man to give her a lift and there will always be guys who...All right, if you say so, I must have took pity on her one night and drove her home. I guess she dropped it."

"Dupree, a woman doesn't just drop a bra off her body."

He had laughed then. Looked up at the moon and laughed although there was nothing particularly funny about the situation. Still, in that moment, it had struck him that he'd rather talk nonsense with her than have intelligent discourse with anyone else on this earth.

"Clio," he said. "I'd swear it with my last breath. I stand before you as an honest man saying that I don't know how that pinky red bra got in the floor of my truck. If you say it was that silly Jeannie girl's to lose, then I'll bow to your greater knowledge. But I never took it off her, if that's what you've spent sixty years thinking and I wasn't there when she took it off herself." He paused. His voice softened. "She might have a had a little crush."

"Oh, she did."

"So then she might have left it deliberate. Hell, I don't know. Giving me some sort of sign to what she was willing to do." He turned towards her shadowy figure. "Are you telling me that's what sent you to the arms of Brian Elliott, nothing more than a red bra lying in the floor of a pick-up truck?"

"Well, that and the fact he was rich."

They had both laughed then. Laughed with that kind of wild desperation you get when you know a story has almost come to its end and it's up to you to tell yourself what it was about. Him and Clio- in the end, the truth doesn't have all that much to do with what really happened. In the end, the truth ain't nothing more than whatever version of the story you've decided you can live with.

She had turned her face toward the sky. "There's a third reason I married Brian. The bra and the sand castle and something else."

"Go on. If we're gonna stand here at this belated date and tell it, we may as well tell it all."

"It was mostly Merry. She was born the day before Christmas, after Brian and I got married in July. My mother in law tried to pass it off that she'd come early but hell, everybody knew she hadn't. There was some shame in the order of things but it was just a small shame, the kind Christians are willing to forgive. We'd gotten married, after all. We'd hustled our way to the altar and done the right thing. Through the years I was just lucky that no one in the family or at the restaurant stopped to remember that Brian didn't even come down to the coast that year until after he graduated Carolina in May."

Now that had stopped him. He'd stooped, tried to look at her face, even though she'd already turned away.

"Hell's bells, Dupree," she'd said. "There I was- married in the heat of summer with a full-term baby girl born the next Christmas. They say this is the most gossipy town in the state. They claim that people start talking about you before you've even had the chance to get out of the room. And yet nearly sixty years passed and you're telling me I'm the only one on Elliott who ever even tried to do the math?"

****

"It didn't surprise me a bit at the memorial," Dupree is saying to Merry. "when you stood up and said you were her daughter. You look just like her."

"Most people say I don't look like anybody."

"Well I say you look like Clio. Or Amy or Josie or Cully or whatever name she was calling herself at that particular point in her life. No mind – just know that looking like your mama is a good thing. Your mama was pretty."

Merry nods. He's old and stooped and evidently half blind as well but there's no need to be rude. Without him they wouldn't have even had a body to lay in the ground. "I never really thanked you for retrieving her. Identifying the...you know. Saving my brother and me that much, at least."

318

"Your Mama and I had been friends when we were young."

"That's what the paper said. It's hard for me to picture her young."

"Really? I never could picture her as anything else. Maybe it's because I first met her when neither one of us was more than a teenager." He stood tall then. Snorted. "She used to come down every year at the start of the summer to work at that restaurant and I drove a produce truck. We started calling her Clio, just to tick her off about that little piss-ant town she was from."

"She never told me that."

"Wouldn't think she would. Course you have to remember this was all before she married your papa, had you and your brothers. Became a great lady. Back when I knew her all she was doing was trying to figure out a way to stay at the beach."

"I can believe that. She loved it here. She used to tell me she loved that view of the point more than she'd ever loved any man."

The old man chuckles. "Reckon that much was true." And it was. All he and Brian

Elliott had ever been doing was vying for second place.

Merry nods. "Now I'm standing here wondering if despite all those years arguing and trying to be anything but, I only managed to wind up just like her. Now that would be a hell of a joke, wouldn't it? If a woman spends a lifetime trying to get away from a place and its memories and she pulls up in a washed out driveway in front of a falling down cottage and all she can think is 'I'm home.'"

They stand for a moment in silence. When the old man finally speaks, his voice is raspy. "I loved your mama."

"God help me, but so did I." Merry looks around. Takes note of the sparkle on the water, the way the sea oats sway in the sand. Even the call of the gulls. They're all down there hopping around on the sand. Angry about something, the way gulls always are.

"It's the last day of summer," she says suddenly. "They say tomorrow's the official start of fall, but I don't know. Feels like there's some summer left out here. Maybe it's just me."

"Nah, I reckon there's a little bit left," says the old man. He has half a mind to hug this woman standing beside him and half a mind to run away. She's wearing slim linen slacks and flat shoes and her hair has been blown dry a certain way that makes her look like an actress in a television commercial. She looks confident. Expensive. Clio tried to tell him something about her, when Merry Elliott was no more than a child. That she liked Miracle Whip better than Duke's, a trivial sort of preference that her mother evidently took as a sign the girl was growing up too full of herself.

Dupree doesn't know about that but he does know that the woman standing before him scares him more than anyone he's ever met. Scares him even more than her terrifying mother. He wonders how much she knows and what, if anything, she might have guessed. Maybe not so much. Never mind. For some reason he senses he will have time enough to get to know her. That she might even be the last and greatest blessing of his life.

But for now she's staring at the rundown cottage, tucked where it's always been, between the dunes. "I told my brother I couldn't wait to get rid of this house."

"And now you're not so sure?"

"Now that I'm actually here, standing in front of it, I'm not so sure of anything." Merry abruptly turns toward Dupree and takes his trembling arm. "As Mama herself would say, Lord, but it's hot. I swung by the Easy Mart on my way in. Maybe I could offer you and your dog a cold drink?"

"Darlin'," he says. "Darlin', I thought you'd never ask."

322

# Acknowledgements

I couldn't have written this book without the support of my writing community, especially my stalwart beta readers Erika Marks, Kabee Kokenes and Katy Jackson. I love you all beyond words!

Special thanks to Bethany Callaway for her beautiful cover design, which not only brought my story to visual life, but exceeded all my dreams. And I am eternally grateful to my PR guru and dear friend Joy Callaway for helping this book find its way in the world. Finally, a big hug goes out to my formatter Leigh Jenkins for being patient with a luddite like me.

But most of all, I'd like to thank my mother Doris Wright Mitchell who forty years ago bought a condo at the sleepy little beach of Cherry Grove, South Carolina and thus changed not only her life but mine and that of my children and grandchildren. The beach holds our family memories and each time I go there I feel, like Cully, every age I've ever been.

Made in the USA
Columbia, SC
22 January 2021